KING PENGUIN

THE ADVENTURES OF
CHRISTIAN ROSY CROSS

David Foster was born in 1944 and spent his early childhood in Katoomba in the Blue Mountains of New South Wales. He trained as a scientist at Sydney University and the Australian National University and spent 1970 in the United States as a Fellow of the National Institute of Health, and 1978 in Europe as recipient of the Marten Bequest for Prose. His novel *The Pure Land* (1974) shared the first *Age* award for the best Australian book of the year, and his novel *Moonlite* (1981) won the National Book Council Award for Australian Literature. He began work on *The Adventures of Christian Rosy Cross* in 1973 and completed it in 1980.

David Foster is married with six children and lives in the southern highlands of New South Wales.

BY THE SAME AUTHOR

North South West
The Pure Land
The Empathy Experiment (with D. Lyall)
Escape to Reality
Moonlite
Plumbum
Dog Rock

DAVID FOSTER

THE ADVENTURES OF CHRISTIAN ROSY CROSS

A KING PENGUIN
PUBLISHED BY PENGUIN BOOKS

Penguin Books Australia Ltd,
487 Maroondah Highway, P.O. Box 257
Ringwood, Victoria 3134, Australia
Penguin Books Ltd,
Harmondsworth, Middlesex, England
Penguin Books,
40 West 23rd Street, New York, N.Y. 10010, U.S.A.
Penguin Books Canada Ltd,
2801 John Street, Markham, Ontario, Canada L3R IB4
Penguin Books (NZ) Ltd,
182-190 Wairau Road, Auckland 10, New Zealand

First published by Penguin Books Australia, 1986

Copyright © David Foster, 1986

All rights reserved. Without limiting the rights under copyright reserved above, no part of this publication may be reproduced, stored in or introduced into a retrieval system, or transmitted, in any form or by any means (electronic, mechanical, photocopying, recording or otherwise), without the prior written permission of both the copyright owner and the above publisher of this book.

Typeset in Garamond Light by Leader Composition Pty Ltd
Made and printed in Great Britain by
Cox and Wyman Ltd., Reading

CIP

Foster, David, 1944– .
The adventures of Christian Rosy Cross.

ISBN 0 14 007701 4.

1. Rosicrucians – Fiction. I. Title.

A823'.3

for Andrew Clegg

ACKNOWLEDGEMENT

This book was written and revised over a ten-year period, from 1973. The financial assistance of the Australian Literature Board during this period is gratefully acknowledged. A radio adaptation of the text, by the author, has been produced for the Australian Broadcasting Commission by Andrew MacLeannan.

CONTENTS

Introduction ix
Christian Rosy Cross 1
Son of Christian Rosy Cross 65
Return of Christian Rosy Cross 129

Introduction

In the early seventeenth century several anonymous pamphlets appeared in Germany, execrating the Pope and purporting to be the work of the Brotherhood of the Rosy Cross. One, *The Chemical Marriage of Christian Rosencreutz*, is an alchemical allegory. Another, the *Fama Fraternitatis*, describes the life of Father Christian Rosy Cross, who travels to the East, acquires wisdom, and returning to Europe founds a Brotherhood. This is a familiar German theme, finding echoes in real life (Paracelsus) no less than myth (Tannhäuser). Whether or not the pamphlets, which differ considerably in tone, were all by the same author, and if so, who that author may have been, is a matter for scholarly debate and not important here. At the time, the pamphlets aroused considerable controversy, with what have become known as Rosicrucian authors stepping in as their apologists. Whether or not the Rosicrucian Brotherhood exists, or should exist if it doesn't, or ever did exist, is a matter for conjecture. Those mystically inclined have seen in the Brotherhood poetic expression of the undeniable existence, at all times in the West, of a gnostic, or hermetic, tradition of heterodoxy, emerging in the Grail legends, alchemy and ceremonial magic, owing much to the Kabbala, but generally subjected before the Reformation to relentless persecution.

Christian Rosy Cross, according to the *Fama*, was born in the year the Church acquired two popes, and died, over a century later, within a year of the birth of Martin Luther. If, as seems likely, he was not an historical figure, he is certainly a symbolic expression of discontent within the Catholic Church, and perhaps an attempt, at the same time, to insinuate the tenets of spiritual alchemy into the fledgling Protestant religion.

A.E. Waite has written extensively on the secret tradition: I have plundered freely his *Lives of the Alchemystical Philosophers* in the following book. The brief excerpts from the pamphlets themselves which appear, are Waite's translation.

What struck me forcibly, after reading Waite's translation of *The Chemical Marriage*, was his observation that when it first appeared in London it was hailed as a 'comic romance'. I reread it, and saw it could be viewed as a kind of 'Sufic satire'; that is, a work superficially satirical, yet incorporating at a structural level those very esoteric elements it purportedly ridicules. Such a work may be offered, with some equanimity, both to friend and foe, and indeed, in its very ambiguity, conforms to Hermetic tradition.

Because of my conviction our present age resembles that of Christian Rosy Cross, I offer the following reconstruction of his life. My mentor in matters alchemical is Michael Maier, and the Latin epigrams which appear in the following book are taken from Maier's works.

David Foster

FOOTNOTE: I interpret the city of Damcar, referred to in the *Fama*, as a variant of Damascus. At the time of Father Rosy Cross' visit, Damascus was under the Mamelukes, an interesting social experiment in empires, run by slaves, with a slave for sultan. This arrangement had the virtue of permitting the native Arabic 'ruling class' time to pursue their enlightened interests, while ensuring that all real imperial power rested in the hands of a group of bloodthirsty ruffians, unperturbed, by any such interests, in their policy formulation. Such a system (though scarcely conceivable to us today) has much to commend it: alas, there is no evidence that Father Christian noticed, and besides, the system was well in decline by the time of his visit.

Christian Rosy Cross

1

Christian Rosy Cross was born in the year of the Great Schism, 1378. He was not like you or me.

The birth: his mother, her face contorted and purple with exertion, pushes down. Christian is still contained by his mother's womb but the midwife can see the colour of his hair. It is black. 'Push' says the midwife: 'keep your elbows off the bed.' Christian's mother is only sixteen. It's her first child and her waters are intact. Christian could end up born in a caul, a highly propitious circumstance. His mother, her contraction over, sinks back on the bed. The room is typically furnished. Christian's head is apparent, but his shoulders pose an impediment. Frightened, exhausted, his mother utters a fearful oath, in two languages.

At once the waters break, drenching the bed, the midwife, the floor. As though on account of his mother's language, Christian will not be born in a caul. Even so, he is not like you or me. As the midwife mops up the straw-coloured fluid, the final contraction occurs.

Christian, blue with blood and white with natal grease, head tapered like an ape's and nose flattened, is thrust forth. The midwife grabs him as he ejects a coil of urine from his penis. It feels good. The midwife bisects the cord and assists with the mother's afterbirth. It is drawn forth like a demon's entrail. Upended and vigorously pummelled by the midwife, the child cries.

'A baby boy' exclaims the midwife.

'Christian' says his mother, 'Christian Rosencreutz.'

Out the window with the afterbirth: here is our body's most amazing organ, a harder worker than the liver. It is not of our mother, this purple robe that mediates life before birth, it is us.

Part of us dies, that we may be born. 'We' (the foetus with the nervous system) are just one part of an ongoing concern and a less efficient parasite than afterbirth to boot. In courtyard now, as pig's snout rips cancer's tutor/barber's pole, Christian's afterbirth expires to no regrets. How unjust: in penetrating women, the copulatory organ is comparatively amateur.

1378. Europe is not as it is now. There are no factories. There is no science, as we understand it. There is no sanitation, as we understand it. Rats and mice, as we understand them, are created *ex nihilo* from piles of dung and rubbish, while germs, as we know them, do not exist. Even so, disease exists: dropsy, plague, pox, leprosy, king's evil. Giving birth is dangerous. Living is dangerous too, but dying is most dangerous, as Heaven and Hell still exist. Life has meaning. There is much illicit sex, and a lot of eating, on a grand scale. There is a lot of drinking, on a grand scale. Jacobus Molay, the last Knight Templar, was burnt at the stake fifty years ago, and old visionaries can still be found who remember St John on the rocks of Patmos ankle deep in coriander finishing off the vulgate. They are good days, these early days, because the *ros,* the dew of reality, is still on the earth, even the earth of Europe.

Christian's mother, having given birth in the absence of ritual, feels depressed. Her baby is taken by the midwife, washed, wrapped in a swaddling cloth and left in a cradle. Christian is born in a castle, and is left to lie in a room of the castle, with his mother, depressed, nearby; but of that castle and depression, more anon.

Wrong birth is like wrong death; events about which our frame of life is builded, pillars of our temple Jakin and Bohaz; yet we trifle with them. Compare the face of a woman in orgasm with the face of a woman giving birth, the face of a woman dying – shouldn't she be laughing not making those awful grimaces?

Christian's putative father, Comte de Rosencreutz, returns from fighting in a war to see Christian, a few hours old, staring at the ceiling in a chamber on the high side of the castle. At this, he turns to his wife. The sight of her, pale, legs apart, arouses emotion in the count. Full of recent gore and bloody deeds, he falls on the countess; the red slave takes a white bride; and the wounds of the woman's childbirth, scarcely healed, are opened afresh.

When it's over, and it doesn't take long, the count asks the countess to account for the child. He's pretty certain he's been away almost a year.

'What do you mean?' replies the countess. 'That child is your child!'

In fact, reviewing the circumstances, she can't think whose child it could possibly be. It's wartime – you understand.

Well, the count stands up and walks to the cradle. He's an old count, forty-odd, and has worn out several wives. Something about the boy takes his fancy. He studies the child from various aspects, while the countess tries to staunch her blood. The blood that has nurtured Christian runs out, soaking the straw in the vicinity. Christian meantime gazes at the ceiling with a placid smile on his face.

Portavit illud ventus in ventre suo.

This is no child of mine, thinks the count.

'Perfidious brachet! The child resembles neither of us! Look at the colour in his hair! Look at the colour in his skin!'

He's about to use his sword on the countess when a number of ladies-in-waiting, roused by the racket, enter the chamber and hurry her off. She dies later in the day of haemorrhage.

Comte de Rosencreutz can't decide whether Christian is his natural son or not. The more he looks, the less certain he grows. Christian's colour is due to jaundice; his hair, however, remains black. Long after the countess dies, the count stands looking at Christian. He looks at the crib, then looks at the blood-soaked straw.

He decides to pray to God.

But God in His wisdom won't guide the count. So the count postpones a decision. When people ask about the child, the count won't answer. He has other children, and within a week, more pressing matters to concern him.

So Christian, the Child of his Age, lives on in a sunlit room on the high side of the castle, attended by ladies-in-waiting. In such consists his early childhood. His father becomes very poor after the death of his mother, because of bad luck with tenants, which is why commentators always say of Christian that he comes from a poor, but noble, family.

Which is better than being rich and working class.

2

At the age of five Christian is taken to a nearby Dominican cloister. What a strange place; everyone dressed up as girls.

In dispensation of monastic observance each monk has his own room. That makes twenty-two rooms in all. One is vacant, and Christian goes in there. It's no school as such; Christian has been taken in reparation for debts the cloister owes his father. An extraordinary meeting is convened after prayers the afternoon Christian arrives. Twenty-one monks and *conversi* (lay brothers), including the prior, are present. Christian is introduced to everyone in turn, but forgets each name as the next is pronounced, so that only the name of the last and least brother, P.A.L., remains with him.

P.A.L. That's Brother Pal, for short.

'This is our young charge Christian Rosencreutz' says the prior, who's also conventual doctor. 'He's to be regarded as an orphan of some social standing. The question is, what to do with him?'

After discussion, Christian is asked what he himself would like to do. For though there'll be lessons in Latin, Greek and Scripture, there'll still be time for menial work.

'I'd like to help the brother who washes the clothes' he replies.

The prior turns pale, but concurs with this request.

'Brother Pal. Fine. Any other requests, Christian?'

'I'd like a few pets to play with.'

'And what sort of pets do you prefer? Our yard is rather small.'

'Toads and eagles best' replies Christian. 'Goats and wolves next best.'

The prior turns more pale still.

'And why do you prefer those animals, Christian? What's wrong with dogs and cats?'

'Those are the animals I had back home' explains Christian. 'The toads lived in the mud where I played and the eagles flew out of the high woods, where they had their nest on the mountain. A goat was my mother, and a wolf killed the dog I regarded as my best friend.'

'I take your meaning' replies the prior. 'Come with me, Christian.'

The prior rises and hastens from the room.

Young boy and old man flap along the flags.

'What are you like at catching toads, Christian?'

'Not bad' says Christian, 'not bad at all.'

'Then go in the yard and catch one, will you? And when you've caught it, bring it to my rooms.'

Christian goes straight to the yard near the laundry and catches a toad. He returns to find the prior trembling and holding a small golden chain in his hand.

'I took this from a chasuble' explains the prior. 'Now let's take a look at that toad of yours. I want to put this chain round its neck.'

'Why?' says Christian.

'Well, it could be a sort of lead, if you like. The other end should be tied to an eagle.'

'But an eagle would pull the toad in the air!'

'Not at all! The toad won't leave the earth, you see, it keeps the eagle in check. Take my meaning, Christian?'

'Not really. An eagle is stronger than a toad.'

'You think hard about what I've said.'

'You're breaking my toad's neck, Prior. That chain is far too tight. I don't want my toad chained up anyway. It walks too slowly for a lead. I'd be dragging it round all the time.'

'What does that matter? Look, it's for the toad's benefit. Try to see things more deeply.'

'I like to see toads undisturbed.'

'Well I don't, Christian; no more does God. He has noosed

us all with His *cathena aurea*, golden chain to the vulgar. Take this golden chain and think about its meaning.'

'Right' says Christian, appraising the item and trying to gauge its worth.

'As far as my other duties permit' says the prior, 'I propose to instruct you myself. You seem a nacreous boy. A hot man, of course, is better than a cold one.'

'Look! The toad wants to go out.'

'Take it out by all means. *Leave* it out. For there, in its natural surroundings, it will learn what God intended it to.'

'And what was that?'

'Couldn't say. Don't know about toads. Men are my speciality. Who can say in whose image a toad was made? Tomorrow, early, I'll baptise you. In the meantime, go and help Brother Pal. Oh, ah Christian: one last thing.'

'Sir?'

'The gold should be inside.'

The baptism of Christian Rosy Cross, 1383. The prior takes him from his room in the morning, while it's still dark. He gives Christian a cassock to wear and says: 'Don't make any noise now. This has to be done before sunrise to mean anything, and I don't want anyone else about. I'm going to try something *meaningful* for once. I wish it were a week before Pentecost.'

Christian observes, as they walk along the flags, that the prior is very agitated.

'What's the matter with you?' he inquires, in his normal, forthright manner.

'I don't know Christian. A little tired, maybe. I've been up most of the night. So many trips to chapel. Still, I don't want the others to know, they mightn't understand. And if they did understand, they mightn't approve.'

The prior opens the chapel door and sets down the candles.

'The font wasn't big enough. I had to borrow a tub from the laundry.'

He leads Christian to the tub, which is set in front of the altar.

In the tub, reflected in candlelight, is what appears to be a dull, silver mirror.

'I'm going to pray now, Christian. You stand there and don't make any noise. There's no point in you praying, until you're baptised it won't mean a thing. I got the stuff in the tub from a friar. He doesn't know what I'm going to use it for, and wants it back this afternoon. Essential to his researches. Take off your cassock if you like. I won't be a minute.'

'My feet are cold' complains Christian.

'Use the chalice on the table; we'll empty it out later. Can't risk going outside.'

While the prior kneels at the rail in prayer, Christian walks to the sanctuary. He doffs his cassock and takes the chalice, which is large, gold and studded with rubies. Not knowing what to do when he's finished with the chalice, he puts it back on the altar.

The prior rises from his attitude of prayer and walks across to the window. The window is of leaded glass and features a horseman from the Apocalypse. At 4 a.m., there is no light.

'I asked God to guide me' says the prior. 'A river would have been best. Baptism, to be meaningful, should take place in a life-giving stream. A river like the Jordan or Nile. I went down town last night to take a look at the stream there, but it's quite unsuitable. Never floods since they put the weir in, which means it doesn't give life to the earth. Water and earth, Christian – take my meaning?'

'Mud' says Christian.

'Ah, you're so perceptive. And from what else does life spring? Toads, if my memory serves me correct, are generated by means of putrefaction in wet dust. Frogs, by contrast, are made in the clouds. Scorpions are made from rotting basilisks, bees from calves, wasps from asses, beetles from horses and locusts from mules. But toads come from the mud itself, which is the critical thing about them, as you say. Wise beyond your years, and that's why you must have a *meaningful* baptism. God has sent you here to me, as a sort of test of my abilities. What luck, what opportunity.'

The prior immerses his fingers in the font.

'Water from the well. I mean to say. Where's the significance in that?'

He walks to the tub.

'Mercury! I got it from Friar Cornelius. He makes it from rocks.'

Christian walks to the tub and looks in. The metal hovers like a wingless bird, its quivering meniscus like a pregnant belly.

'Watch this' says the prior. He removes his ring and drops it in the tub. The mercury gobbles the ring like a lion.

'Incredible stuff, Christian. That ring is now gone forever. This is the most precious stuff in the world. The vapours go up, and the vapours come down. It contains sulphur, or seed of gold. Ah, if only there were some way of making that seed *grow*! For once it were turned to gold, they say, there would be no reconverting it. Frankly, I can't see how that could be, but it makes a wonderful symbol. It is fire, earth, water, air, all in the one tub. Hop in.'

Christian hops in the tub; the mercury bears his weight. The prior forces him onto his back, and begins to splash the mercury on him, intoning as he does: 'I baptise you in the name of God the Father, God the Son and God the Holy Ghost, in the name of Adam, Moses, Daniel, Solomon, St John, in the name of Hermes and in the name of Christ.'

The tub is ruined through amalgamation.

A day later Christian begins to tremble. After baptism he can't hold a quill, can't draw a straight line.

'What's the matter with you?' asks the prior. 'You're making no progress at all!'

But Christian can neither speak, read nor write. He starts to throw fits. His skin turns a funny brown colour, and his brain harbours sensual visions.

The worried monks put the child to bed. Some are convinced he is catching the plague, others, that he is possessed of the Devil.

Monks meet round the bed in which Christian tosses and moans, to discuss the matter. Cornelius turns up a bit late, smelling of brimstone, but guesses at once. He has seen retired workers from the Spanish mercury mines.

Will Christian recover? The prior, distraught as well as contrite, thinks God is repossessing the boy.

'The mercury has made him ill' says Cornelius. 'It penetrates and permeates all parts of the body, and within the body conjugates. There's only one hope.'

'Yes?'

'It must be sweated out! Let's make a steam bath. But if he recovers, he's *mine*, you understand? Mine, from this day on!'

'Of course' says the prior. It does no harm to let Cornelius think what he will.

The friar is back within the hour. 'Consulting my horoscope' he says, 'I find Saturn in opposition to Sol. What do you think of that?'

'I don't know' replies the prior. 'But whether Christian lives or dies, there must be hope. What is the spiritual situation of a man drowned in a baptismal tub? I confess I find him a thought-provoking brat.'

Cornelius takes Christian to the kitchen and puts him in a bed with white sheets, covering him well so he's not suffocated by smoke from the nearby furnace. He gives him water to drink in such copious amounts the boy begins to sweat; the white sheets are stained with an evil black residuum.

'The mercury has dissolved throughout his body' infers Cornelius, grimly.

'Oh no' says the prior, wringing his hands.' How *could* I have been so stupid?'

After a few days, the sheets Brother Pal is constantly washing to monitor progress are clean as a whistle. No further mercury can sweat its way out, so Christian is placed in another bed, bolstered with the feathers of a young black eagle and pillowed with the feathers of an old white swan.

On the bed Cornelius lays a black cassock, with a white surplice for a cover. Christian is installed, and the bed sealed up, so neither sweat nor vapour can escape.

'You'll kill him' expostulates the prior. 'The child will suffocate in there!'

'We have to take that chance' explains Cornelius.

The bed is heated from below and Friar Cornelius rubs

Christian's body with a potent unguent prepared from the genitals of an unspecified animal. Black bile begins to ooze from about the boy's temples.

Yet all is well: the change in colour reveals that Christian is losing and regaining consciousness. He is now black, now white, now red.

The treatment is continued a further three days, and on the morning of the third day the monks awake to find a great change come over Christian. He looks much better.

Cautiously the prior opens Christian's mouth, and peers inside.

Success! The palate is white no longer.

Christian is returned to the infirmary, where the prior, to express thanks, anoints the boy's body with water and oil mixed with sulphur and wine, and pronounces benediction.

Completely recovered, Christian finds himself strong as ever he's been. What is more, all the monks have taken him to their hearts.

3

The prior and Cornelius work as a team to effect Christian's education, for in things spiritual he shows little interest; if the liturgy gets dull he walks out. It's hard for a monk to cavil at this.

The monks, though Christian annoys and irritates them, love the boy dearly. They talk about him behind his back, a sure sign they're learning something from him.

Cornelius takes Christian into his room, anxious to introduce him to the *Art*. The room is kept locked, so no one can enter; it's a secret room. From time to time, over the years, Cornelius has introduced other novices, but none has proven suitable. None has shown aptitude. Cornelius has grown rather weary and cynical, for the *Work* is more than one man can handle, and has stubbornly refused to yield its mysteries to him. But perhaps with the right assistant. The sages unanimously recommend engaging a female, a *soror mystica*, but these days most adepts live in cloisters, so that's out of the question.

Against one wall of the secret laboratory is the laboratory proper.

The whole room is actually the laboratory, but the furnace is set in the wall, and most of the laboratory is scattered around the furnace. The furnace enclosure looks like three-quarters of a four-poster bed, one side and both ends. Chimneywork reaches to the ceiling, beginning against the wall ten feet off the floor and resting upon four columns of the Doric order, the two furthermost flush against the wall. Hiding the contents of the enclave are three curtains, stretching from column to column. Upon the stylobate of the two nearer columns is written '*Ratio*' and '*Experientia*'. On the frieze is written '*Solve*'. A clenched fist thrusts index and middle fingers into the air. Upon the projecting cornice rest many glazed bottles and containers, marked from the left: 'hyle' 'sang' 'azoth' 'green ultramontane atrament' 'sal gemmae' 'eagle salts' 'alum zuchinarum' 'urine' 'vinegar' 'crocus water' 'iron filings' 'father of sublimate' 'egg oil' 'millet' 'our arsenic' 'bombax' – and many others. Interspersed among these are bits of metal and ore, dusty and sulphurous, and everywhere lumps of lead, fallen from the monastery roof.

On the curtains, which are frayed and filled with holes from hot objects, are many interesting symbols, hand-woven. Friar Cornelius opens the curtains and watches as Christian explores the precincts. Scattered around the floor are cucurbits, lutes, bottles and phials. A large pair of bellows lays by the furnace gate, together with a tub of coals. From another tub issues the odour of horse dung. This, mixed with the odour of sulphur, dominates the room. Droplets of mercury hang from every surface, fill every crevice. Glass vessels, retorts and filters, brazen mortars and pots, clay jars, ironware tools, alembics and aludels; in one corner, a philosophical egg.

Christian is suitably impressed. He burns himself on a hot pipe, spills a jar of stinking water, moistens one finger and dissolves with his touch a feather of alum on the bench; it tastes like the bleached bones of a great, extinct seabird. Within the furnace can be made fierce fire, suitable for smelting ores. But the fierce fire is not raging. A gentle fire burns instead. Friar Cornelius is trying to refurbish some damaged apparatus. He opens the furnace and removes, with tongs and tweezers, a pestle and a crucible to which some matter adheres. He strikes the one against the other, to no avail. The hardened matter stays fast. With trembling hands he replaces the pestle, leaving the crucible on the bench.

In sudden despair, he shouts.

Orbita quadruplex hoc regit ignis opus.

'You have here Christian, the fierce and fiercer fire. In the yard is my cinnabar room, that room next to the laundry in which I distil mercury, the room with the lock you've been trying to break ever since you arrived here. Well of course, I can give you the key now.'

He produces a key and replaces it.

'Some other time. But remember, trying to get into the cinnabar room without a key is like trying to walk without feet. At the moment I'm working on the *Vegetable Stone*. I've given the *Mineral Stone* away. You see, there is another room, and in there, my *Projection*.'

He leads Christian to another room, which contains a vat of horse dung. Sitting in the vat, secured by bossheads and clamps, is another philosophical egg, the *Vas Philosophorum*, seething with matter of indescribable putrescence. Friar Cornelius walks to the vase and inspects its contents, well satisfied.

'Black as coal, Christian. I will shortly commence the next operation, and you can help me.'

Christian approaches the vase, and looks in. Month-old yolks from 2,000 hen eggs.

'Well' says Cornelius, 'what's the verdict?'

'I like it' says Christian. 'I'm taken with the place.'

Friar Cornelius speaks on, discursively.

'I used to smelt my ores in here, but the heat became too much for the woodwork. So I put in a room out back. Then, when visiting Cologne, I struck my present set-up in a disused wing of the old convent. It belonged to Albert, our provincial at one time. *Albertus Magnus*, a great adept. 'From an ass to a philosopher and back to an ass, with the help of the Virgin's Milk.'

'After matins' says the prior to Christian, 'I want you go come to my rooms.'

'For a lesson?'

'Yes' says the prior. 'But not in reading or writing.'

'You like that smelly place' says the prior. 'Still, what boy would not. Even so, there is something I must impress upon you. Please don't get me wrong; I'm glad you'll be working with Friar Cornelius, he has much useful knowledge. Supposing you wish to become an apothecary, or tinsmith, or glassblower. But let me ask you this: do you know what he's looking for?'

'No' says Christian.

'Neither does he. And what's more, if he did, he wouldn't find it.'

The prior takes an old letter from his desk and reads it aloud.

' "The prior. Sir. Having learnt of your fame, I desire to make known my progress to date, in the hope and expectation you will let me join your order.

' "I was born heir to a noble family, my father a distinguished physician. I became a votary of the *Goldmaker's Art* at an early age, and quite by chance. As a youth, my father sent me to a man to be instructed in the *artes liberales*, but my tutor, unbeknown to my father, was a devotee of the *Magisterium*. He inspired me with his enthusiasm" ' – here the prior casts a meaningful glance, only to find Christian staring out the window – ' "so we speedily abandoned quadrivium and trivium, in order to further our acquaintance with Nature. I went to Toulouse to study law, still with my tutor, where we spent the money I had for our maintenance buying furnaces, instruments and drugs, in the hope of following the recipes of the sages, and thereby repaying the money one hundredfold. Instead, my tutor died of a fever he contracted during summer, which misfortune I blame on the attention he paid to the furnace he'd erected in his chambers. His death had a profound effect on me, because my father, learning of my defections, refused to pay me any more money than was thereafter needed except for my subsistence. On coming of age, I returned home and immediately sold some of my property for 400 crowns. I need this money to pursue a process given me in Toulouse by an Italian, who said he has seen it proven.

' "We dissolved gold and silver in various strong waters, but to no avail. We could not recover from solution one half of our gold and silver. Of my 400 crowns barely 200 remained, some of which I gave to the Italian, as he wanted to return to Milan to check certain aspects of the process with its author.

I have not seen him since.

' "In the following summer the city was visited by the plague, and I went to Bordeaux to practise my profession. I did not, however, lose sight of my real ends, and on meeting a philosopher who had a process he thought certain to succeed, I again abandoned myself to the *Art*, until such time as my money was spent. To continue my operations with more certainty, I made the acquaintance of a friar who lived near the city, a man obsessed with the same pursuit as myself, who had just been sent a process from a cardinal in Rome. He estimated it would cost 200 crowns, of which I was to supply half. The process required a large supply of spirits of wine. I purchased several casks of the most excellent wine, and in the course of two years we rectified the spirits more than thirty times till we could not find glasses strong enough to hold them. We then took two pounds weight of spirits, and half a pound weight of gold, which we calcined for a month. The result we included in a pelican and placed in the furnace. Our fire occupied us continually, but we made other experiments in the meantime, for amusement.

' "After a year there was no sign of the *Midnight Sun of Apuleius*, and I believe there would not be, to this day. Nonetheless, we took our powder, and made projection on to hot quicksilver. This way we lost all the gold we might otherwise have recovered.

' "I then sold all but a portion of my property for 800 crowns, and set off for Paris, where there are more adherents to the *Margarita Pretiosa* than anywhere else in the world. My bad luck could not make me desist, and I resolved to stay in Paris until I had succeeded, or until my money was all spent. I made my family think I intended to purchase a situation at the law courts.

' "Once established in Paris, I became acquainted with over a hundred artists like myself, most of whom I met at the furnace makers. Many were labouring to extract mercury of metal, and afterwards to fix it. I am ashamed to admit we visited one another on Sundays, to see what progress had been made.

' "None. 'Would that my vessel had been strong enough to

resist the force of what it contained' etc. I rapidly spent my money, most notably on an expensive process with cinnabar which failed. However, in the course of it, I developed considerable skill with mercury. As to the *Donum Dei*, I succeeded no better than before.

' "My money gone, I returned to that little of the family estate which remained. By disposing of all deeds and titles I was able to raise enough money to buy what was necessary, and once again began upon my operations, in an atmosphere of solitude and tranquillity marred only by the attitude of my family – consisting by this stage of my invalid mother and twin sister – who asked had I not lost enough through my folly. My mother was afraid if I continued to purchase so much coal I should be suspected of counterfeiting coin. However, I found no consolation but in my work, to which I gave my undivided attention. The interruption of all commerce in the district occasioned by plague, however, caused me to journey to Spain to obtain cinnabar, and when I returned I found my sister had come in my chamber in my absence, and broken my furnaces in pieces!

' "I raved, and cried bitterly. For over a week I sat morosely surveying the wreckage. Then, in the corner, I noticed something which, in the nature of such things, had escaped my attention. A piece of lead, cylindrical, curiously and suggestively shaped, about five inches in circumference and six or eight inches long, which must have fallen from the wall, had been entirely converted to gold! I assayed it at more than twenty-four carats. I searched intently, but there was no more. In the wrecking of my lab, my sister had spontaneously created the tincture – but by what means, and in what combination?

' "I made a careful list of all materials present in my lab, and this I vow will never leave my person. It is a comprehensive list; the room served as my kitchen and privy; but insofar as my search has been narrowed, I can only gives thanks to God. If I now sell all that has fallen to my estate – my mother and sister having recently departed – I again have enough to buy what I need and travel to your cloister, if you will have me. It goes without saying I'm a most devout man. Yours sincerely etc." '

The prior sighs, puts down the letter. 'I took him in, notwithstanding. We needed a lawyer at the time. Your father was threatening to sequester the monastery. But Cornelius, as it turned out, was useless in that respect as well. He knew very little law. His sister subsequently wrote to him reclaiming her ornament, but he refused to reply.'

'What about my father?'

'I owed him money, Christian, and I have a confession to make: I was once a martyr to the *Circean Art*, as hard a case as Cornelius. I even enjoyed a small reputation. But I saw the light, and want you to see it.'

'So I achieved what Cornelius could not?' says Christian, after some thought.

'In the matter of your father? Yes, I guess so. But you do see the point I'm trying to make?'

'No' says Christian, 'I can't say I do.'

The prior leans forward, eyes shining. 'Christian' he says 'the *Vas Philosophorum* is not a flask, but the soul of man! For whether is greater? The gold, or the temple that sanctifieth the gold?'

'I'll bear that in mind' says Christian. 'May I be excused? I want to get back to the lab.'

'It was an accident' concedes Cornelius, 'but out of my lab he stays! My precious tincture, soaking in the dung! My neonatal phoenix shattered!'

'It never worked before' says the prior.

'Last time he let the fire go out and rekindled it with grease.'

'He's only eight' explains the prior. 'Give him a go. It's not his fault.'

4

In 1390 the prior returns from his chapter meeting with bad news. Christian, now twelve, is making good progress, if not in chemistry. Cornelius has been dead two years, and the secret lab is locked.

'The end of a lifestyle' moans the prior. 'Our new master, Raymond of Capua, has revoked the spirit of our constitution, and reintroduced monastic observance. He intends to establish in each province a convent of especially strict regime and I need not add we were elected, save for my single dissenting vote.'

'What's monastic observance?' asks Christian.

'It means' says the prior, 'we sleep on hard beds in a dormitory like schoolboys; we practice total abstinence; we fast every Friday and from September till Easter; we speak only when spoken to, and live by alms. And that's not all. Apostasy and heresy outside these walls have come to the attention of the Pope. He intends to establish an arm of the Inquisition in this very province. I was accordingly instructed by Raymond to release as many friars as possible to assist our Roman brothers, when they appear, as agents of the Holy See. Don't all volunteer at once.'

'Most unwise' says a fat friar. 'Plebs are in an ugly mood. When I was in town the other day some hoodlums threw stones at me and called me a black bastard.'

'There'll be repercussions' says the prior. 'We're none of us safe now.'

'What's the Inquisition?' asks Christian.

'Never you mind' says the prior. 'You and I are staying here, that's one thing for certain. We can't neglect your education, and I have to complete my commentaries on Maimonides in the Thomistic style. I've a portrait of Thomas hanging in my room, you know.'

'And I don't like the look of him' says Christian.

'What? The greatest man our order produced! How dare you say such a thing!'

'He was too fat' says Christian. The monks laugh, for their learned prior is no thinner.

'Will you be going to the Inquisition' Christian asks Pal.

'I'm not a priest' says Pal. 'I'm a lay brother. Someone brings in the laundry, and you and I wash it.'

'What made you come here in the first place?' says Christian. 'It's not much of a life. I'm getting out as soon as I can, but don't tell the prior.'

'I don't want to discuss it, Christian. Hand me that sheet.'

'Is Brother Pal an heretic?'

The prior leans across the desk and grabs Christian's scapula.

'Now listen, Christian, you drop this business! You'll get Brother Pal in a whole lot of trouble! All right, what's on the agenda? I've been away and forgotten where we were.'

'You were going to give me the history of our order.'

'Was I? Well as you know we're all scholars, and you could become a doctor like me. I'd like you to study at the *Studium Generale* in Cologne. Meister Eckhart taught there, now there's an interesting man. Vicar of Bohemia, and they called him an heretic. It makes you wonder who's next.'

'I've always thought you had special qualities Christian, I don't know what they are. You don't seem to have much flair for languages, but we'll send you off to the *Studium*, and hope you become enlightened.'

The prior gets up, starts pacing about. He's aged a great deal in the past few months.

'Actually, it's an appropriate time to tell you about our order. What with this pair of popes excommunicating between them the whole of Christendom, a young man soon to be ordained should realize it wasn't always so.

'Our story begins in Languedoc, in 1216. There were people who believed in two Gods, in the city at that time.'

'Like two popes?' offers Christian.

'One was the God of Light, the Good God.'

'Pope Boniface.'

'One was the God of Darkness, the Evil God.'

'Pope Clement.'

'Christian, will you please shut up? The idea was that the world was made by the Evil God, and Christ, the son of the Good God, was sent to redeem the world.'

'Hey, that's a good explanation' says Christian.

'It is not, it's wrong! The world is not evil but good. The God of the philosopher is the God of the commentator. Now where was I?'

'Languedoc.'

'Ah yes. These men of Languedoc, so-called *cathari*, rejected the Church and all the sacraments. What could we do? Can't very well excommunicate people who reject the system entirely.'

'Turn the other cheek?'

'What? And let them lead others astray? Their priests, the so-called *perfecti*, were very learned in argument. Dominic, who was a young man then, saw the danger in the situation. So disgusted was he when he saw that these heretics could baffle with their specious argument all the stupid cathedral clergy and Benedictine monks, he thought; it won't do. There is a need, in the Church, for men who can argue the case logically and clearly, and who can practise what they preach. So he established our order to preach the truth and live it.'

'We preach the truth and live it?'

'We try to preach it, in any event.'

'But we never go outside!'

'We have to know what the truth is, first!'

'I thought the truth was in Scripture. Why not preach the Scripture?'

'A very Franciscan viewpoint. Because people get sick and

tired of Scripture. Besides, seeing they see not, and hearing they hear not, neither do they understand. Certainly the truth is in Scripture, but it's also in the world outside. You see, when you're arguing with heretics who know their Scripture better than you, you get involved in all sorts of arguments over interpretation. The best idea is to have some completely knock-down, secular arguments. We believe in reason.'

'And did Dominic's arguments work in Languedoc?'

'He had to call in the Crusaders.'

A few weeks later there's knocking at the gate in the early hours of the morning. Christian opens up.

It's not the laundry basket. In the grey of morning, one man in a white habit stands in front of a dozen men in grey. Behind them, mutter the secular arm. It is the Inquisition.

The man in white steps forward. 'How do you do' he says. 'I am Raymond, master of your order. Take me to your prior, please.'

'He's not expecting you' says Christian.

Nice style of a boy, thinks the master.

'Live in expectancy, my son. We may be put in the scales any time, and if found wanting ... what's your name?'

'Christian.'

'Take me to your prior, Christian. I guess he's praying in chapel.'

Roused from bed, the prior stands in his nightshirt rubbing his eyes.

'The Angelic Doctor' says Raymond, looking at the portrait on the wall. 'I wonder if this comfortable room would have met with his approval.'

'I think hrrr' wheezes the prior, 'he would not hrrr have enjoyed the hrrr hrrr hrrr spectacle of grey friars in this house.'

'Perhaps you're right' says Raymond. 'And perhaps you'll favour us with a tour of inspection. We're looking forward to seeing a strict convent's daily operations.'

'We're not strict yet' says Christian. 'Haven't had the time.'

'I take it you've come for those monks' says the prior.

'In a manner of speaking' says Raymond. 'I thought I'd start my Inquisition here. Begin at the seat of the cancer.'

He waves his arm and the party departs. The prior sits immobilized.

'You know Christian, I never thought this could happen to me.'

'Oh well' says Christian, 'a tour of inspection's nothing to worry about.'

The prior laughs.

'What's that' asks Raymond.

'A room' says the prior, 'designed and built for smelting ores.'

'No one desires to smelt ores' says Raymond, 'except to make gold. I've seen enough. This cloister is a disgrace to God and the Order of the Preachers, and I'm satisfied you've made no attempt to withdraw monastic dispensation. I note the absence of the communal dormitory. I note the wine cellar and the size of the goblets. I note the succulent viands in the larder.'

'We're scholars' says the prior, 'we need good sustenance!'

'Scholarship cannot bring us to God' says Raymond. 'Dealbate Latonam & rumpite libros!'

'Apostate' shouts the prior. 'Antimaster! Who voted you in? How dare you come here in the name of Dominic? You're nothing but a Franciscan in disguise!'

A grey monk shuffles forward at this, waving a piece of vellum.

'We have the papal imprimatur to purge the mendicant orders . . .'

'Shut up' says the prior. 'I know your kind!'

'You should do' replies the Franciscan. 'You've sent enough of us to the stake, for daring to expose your venality!'

'He's right' shouts Raymond. 'We must reimpose the spirit of apostolic poverty!'

Christian wonders what's going on. Who's right? Who's wrong? What's the argument?

'Call in the secular arm' says Raymond. 'We've wasted enough time here. We'll tidy this place up, starting with the lab and distillery on the second floor.'

'Please no' implores Christian, who hopes to inherit the glassware.

'Christian, you fool, this is no way to make gold!'

'Could you please spare me the egg?'

'We'll see.'

While the secular arm is smashing the lab, the prior and Christian sit outside. It's a clear, sunny day but the yard is rather shady. Exploding glassware; the sound of birds.

The prior has a strange, manic expression on his face.

'Are you listening Christian? They're going to burn me, I suppose you can see that, can you? It's in my power to prevent it, all I have to do is lie. I was an Inquisitor once, you know. I sent several young Italian friars to the stake for insisting the Pope was the Antipope. How right they were.'

Beyond the wall sits a vulture. 'I am the white of the black' it is singing, 'and the black of the white, and am found in the valleys and on the mountains, and am very truthful.'

5

Raymond the Inquisitor sits at the table, before him a copy of the gospels. Around the court are secular familiars, to guard him and his grey friars.

'Heretics' says Raymond, 'fall in six categories: perfect heretics, who avow heresy and model their lives upon it; lapsed heretics, who return like dogs to their vomit; penitent heretics, who *were* obstinate, but satisfactorily recant; negative heretics, heretical by chance; positive heretics, who hold error and reveal it in word and deed; and secret heretics, who hold error but do not reveal or betray it.'

One by one monks and *conversi* come forward attesting their faith, except the prior, who claims the Church is really the Whore of Babylon. Christian, being under fourteen, is not required to testify.

'I take it that's everyone?' says Raymond.

'One is missing' says Christian.

'Toady' shouts a black friar.

'Silence!' orders Raymond. 'By opposing an Inquisitor you prove yourself heretical!'

'I'll find him for you' says Christian.

'He's probably going to give Brother Pal the office to keep hidden' says the prior. 'Christian can be trusted, you can see it in his eyes. You must always trust the body; notice how my asthma's gone?'

Christian looks hard for Brother Pal, but he's not to be found in his usual haunts, or standing in the damage, or outside in the yard. 'Brother Pal' shouts Christian, 'there's nothing here for you to fear!'

Eventually he finds his friend crouching in the disused sewer, with several toads for company, by the dead figs and pomegranates from the abandoned orchard, where leeks and pennyroyal grow wild.

'Why is your name not on my roll?' asks Raymond.
'Ah ah ah . . .' says Pal.
'Clear the court!'
The court is cleared; only Pal and Christian remain.
'Now my friend, begin at the beginning.'
'My lord Inquisitor: I am a penitent, an *immuratus*, sentenced to life by the Holy See. The kindly prior took pity on me and allowed me to live as a lay brother.'
'I see no harm in that' admits Raymond, 'but where are your penitent's crosses? I suggest we go outside; I find the atmosphere rather close. Too much earth and water in here, not enough fire and air.'
'Create equality among the elements' says Christian, 'and you do more than air a room!'
'That's enough of that sort of talk' says Raymond.

'Why were you locked up' says Raymond. A notary takes notes.
'Donatism' says Pal.
'Aha' says Raymond, 'of all heresies, the least culpable. Do you now accept that a rotten, corrupt priest can administer valid sacraments?'
'I do indeed' says Pal.
'Good' says Raymond, 'you've made some progress.'

Brother Pal reabjures, and the prior takes the stand. After hearing charges of heresy and goldmaking, he's asked does he have any enemies.
At this, he laughs.
'I find it hard to extenuate the crime you openly laugh at' says Raymond. 'There is no greater crime than teaching people who can't see, and rely on faith, to worship false images. But

what hurts most of all, is that you had in your charge, not just a cloister full of monks who looked to you for guidance, but a boy you bent to your own predilections, as well as a penitent heretic.

'I could use torture, but why bother? A man should only be condemned through free confession or direct proof.

'The verdict. All stand!

'I am driven, compelled and forced to the conclusion, which no shuffling can alter, that the prior of this cloister is a perfect heretic who frowns at his Inquisitor, and in view of the fact he is obstinate and refuses to return to the bosom of the Church, I decree he be defrocked, and since the Church can have no further dealings with him, abandoned to the secular arm.

'I further find great, strong and forcible arguments that a friar of this cloister recently deceased, Cornelius by cognomen, was a perfect, obnoxious and practising heretic, and I decree his remains to be exhumed from consecrated ground and abandoned, together with his notebooks and as much of his apparatus as remains intact, to the secular arm.

'I find further forcible arguments in the general condition of this cloister, that the religious of this cloister have been heretical in their derelictions, but I allow they may have repented, and decree they be deposed and defrocked and driven from the Order of St Dominic, and further, that they be removed from the cloister to find gainful employment, and further, that they wear the crosses as described in the decree of Toulouse, one on their breast and one on their back, of a colour different to their clothes, and wearing those crosses at all times, shall appear in church every Sunday, where being stripped, or insofar as the weather will permit, they are to be beaten by the priest, publicly, between the reading of the epistle and the gospel.

'I find the *immuratus* guilty of no fresh error, and decree he is to suffer no penalty for the heresy of his jailors, which he abhors. But he is to wear his crosses.

'Last and not least, I find this cloister so far fallen into error, and so far departed from the spirit of its founder, that I am giving it, by way of penance, to the Order of the Spiritual

Brothers of St Francis, in the hope they will set an example.'

There are cries of 'Shame' and 'Scandal' at this, but the court is adjourned.

'What will the soldiers do with the prior?' asks Christian.

'Burn him, of course' says the master. 'Fire is a great purifier, and wipes out all error.'

'But the prior is still alive!'

'Only in a manner of speaking. "Peior enim est malus quam bestia" – Thomas Aquinas. An heretic is no better than an animal.'

'I'm a coward, Christian' explains Pal. 'I don't like being tortured. I was led to the stake once, but recanted to save my life. Do you blame me?'

The prior is wearing a tall paper mitre inscribed with the words, *hic est haeresiarcha*.

'Jesu Christe, Fili Dei vivi, miserere mei' he says. 'Jesu Christi, Fili Dei qui passus est pro nobis, miserere mei.'

Next, he prepares to deliver a speech.

Around him is gathered the whole cloister. The air is crisp, it's a crisp mid-autumn midafternoon. An occasional breeze fans the loose habits of the convention, and the air is filled with the scent of crushed bones and burnt paper. On the ground Christian finds a shard of chemical egg, near it a lump of consecrated earth.

'Be warned' says the prior. 'A week ago, as the lab was smashed by the agents of this False Crusade, I became aware of a strange phenomenon. I suddenly felt the gaze of God upon me. For a while I was worried lest it depart, but I soon learned certain patterns of thought and virtuous forms of behaviour ...'

'Same old story' says the master. 'Light the faggots please.'

The secular arm move in and strap the prior to the stake. He starts to speak more hurriedly.

'Christian? Are you listening? We're in the last days of mfph . . . '

'Sorry' says Christian, 'I can't understand.'

'And I've heard enough' says the master. 'He doesn't want to save *his* soul, just wants Christian to lose his. Fire!'

The paper hat is first to go. Third degree burns look bad, but they don't hurt, as the nerve endings are next.

In the meantime, Christian undergoes a peculiar physical change. He falls to the ground, his eyes start, and his limbs begin to twitch. He froths at the mouth, pisses himself, and bites his tongue severely.

'Whoa' shouts Raymond. 'Can't you see what's happening? The evil spirit of the prior is trying to enter the boy! Quick! Drag him to the fire!'

As soon as Christian feels the heat, he smartly comes to his senses. He watches the smoke till the smoke has gone. What an unmanning spectacle.

'There' says Raymond, 'no trace remains. Can those bones live again?'

'The salamander lives in the fire' says Christian, in a deep voice.

'Rubbish' says Raymond. 'You believe that sort of thing, you'll believe anything.'

6

Christian persuades his new masters to let him recommence chemistry. This time, the fire is purely spiritual. The burnt prior's little golden chain, with some mercury, is set aside in the egg, and every day for three years Christian prays for success. After three years he opens up, and finds nothing has happened.

'Blast! I'll never have money for a castle now!' The cloister has changed a great deal, though it's even more boring than before. Monastic observance is strictly obeyed. There's never enough to eat and drink, and everyone has to get up early and work hard all day. Pal's happy: 'We have to be punished' he says, 'because we're sinners.'

'Speak for yourself' says Christian. 'I haven't done a wrong thing in years!'

Everyone else has a guilty conscience; it's nothing for monks to pull out chains and thrash themselves for hours. Idle speech is strictly forbidden. The only person Christian speaks to is Pal, and he knows nothing.

'How do I get out of here?'

'You don't' says Pal. 'Scale the wall, you'll run back in the main gate. I hear the people are starving! If we didn't have our own garden we'd be in a pretty pickle.'

As it is, they live on leeks and lentils. Christian recalls vividly the last Dominican Christmas. Roast beef, mutton, venison, pork, trout, eels, lamprey, shellfish, chickens, pheasants, capons, quail, ducks, wheatcakes, pastries, custards, beers, wines . . .

'Yes, I understand the state of the world approximates that of the Antichrist' says Pal. 'Pestilence abounds, and as for sin, well you've only to look at these sheets.'

'What do you mean, look at these sheets.'
'How old are you now Christian?'
'Fifteen.'
'Fifteen already!'

A few months later, Christian admits to a slight physical problem.
　'Aha' says Pal, smiling, 'about time. Try embrocation. Let me know what happens.'

'Now let me get this straight' says Pal. 'You're troubled by stiffness?'
　'I am' says Christian.
　'Often?'
　'Only the once.'
　'Only the once! That can't be right . . . what exactly have you done?'

'I see. And it didn't work?'
　'Nothing works.'
　'Let's take a look at this offending member.'
　Christian at once unloosens his belt and raises high his cassock.

Later that day, Pal confronts the prior, who's tending lentils in the rain. 'Prior' he says, 'I must speak with you.'
　'It can't wait?'
　'It can't wait.'

'Stay' says the prior, as monks begin leaving chapel after evening prayers. The air is filled with the miasma of wet cloth, hydrogen sulphide, sweat and bloodied flesh.
　'We have a problem' says the prior. 'Christian, be so good as

to demonstrate.'

Christian does; monks gasp.

'Poor lad' observes the prior. 'He's been this way a month. Merely, er, conventional methods afford him no relief.'

'Maybe he doesn't know what to do' says one of the monks, knocking over a pew.

'No. We've something diabolical here. His voice hasn't broken, and there's no pubic hair.'

'Look at this little lady, Christian' says one, indicating a Virgin. 'Does she look different to before?'

Christian studies the statue. 'There's plaster coming off the nose.'

'No' says the prior, 'this is reprobation. The answer is flogging, penance and prayer. I can't believe you're as big a villain as your affliction suggests, Christian, but since you've been chosen to bear the blame, I want you to stay here in chapel. You know what to pray for?'

Christian shrugs. He later finds kneeling affords relief.

The monks are speaking without being spoken to. 'Nice style of boy' they say. 'Not a bit like you or me. There are places where a boy with a build like that . . .'

'Silence!' orders the prior. 'this matter must be resolved! I want you to go about your devotions tonight, with unusual severity.'

'Shall we tell him what it's for?' asks Pal.

'I think not' says the prior. 'To fill his mind with poisonous ideas could worsen his confusion.'

'I wonder if a boy who can't masturbate is meant for monastic life.'

'How dare you! Go to your laundry this minute and say a hundred Hail Marys.'

Christian remains on the sanctuary floor, and looks out through the window. The leaded glass window in the vault is the last left in the cloister.

'I'm getting out of here' thinks Christian. 'Someone will have an answer.'

When the prior observes that Christian's condition is unchanged after a month, he ignores it. Pal remains in the laundry, the prior returns to his garden, and Christian, wearing his black habit, heads for the back wall. There's always the main gate, nailed open, but somehow it doesn't seem right. The year is 1393 and Christian is fifteen years old.

Make haste slowly Christian: wisely tried will succeed once.

7

The Stone is said to be everywhere. Rosarius says in the *Turba*, 'If I were to call the Stone by name, no one would believe me'. And Morienus, 'The Stone is with the rich and the poor, the liberal and avaricious, with those going and those standing still. It is thrown on the roads and trampled on the dunghill, and many have dug in the dirt to dig it up that were disappointed in their expectations.' And Mundus, 'If merchants only knew what they were selling when they were selling the Stone, they would up the ante.' And Arnoldus, 'One can obtain the Stone in abundance, for nothing, whenever one wants, and without having to ask for it.' So it can be sold, yet it is free; it is precious, yet found in the dung; it is in the bad as well as in the good; it is in the earth as well as in the air; it is on the mountains as well as in the rivers; in fact, it owes its origin to Mercury, who gave the Egyptians their laws and religion, and from the Theban priests it spread to the Jews, and to the Greeks, and to the Romans, and from there to the whole world. For that which the wise seek is Mercury and nothing else, it is He who should be searched for until He is found, whether in the air or in the fire, or in the earth or in the water, because He wanders a lot, and likes nothing better than mud and old sewers. But if someone says he has Mercury in his grasp, note that he stands with empty hands and a stupid, tongue-tied expression.

Moving slowly perforce with his legs thrusting forward in a dusty pivotal motion as though walking were not natural to him but an art he had but recently and imperfectly acquired, Christian sees a man approaching from the opposite direction. A man of middle height, in filthy peasant attire. He carries a knapsack tied to a pole, and as Christian reaches him, he unshoulders the pole and opens the sack.

'Would you care to see some filthy woodcuts?' he inquires.
'Sure' says Christian, 'why not?'

'Look at the sun and the moon' says the man. 'Fishing for trout in peculiar streams. Now look at the maimed king. *There's* a nasty disability.'

'I should be so unfortunate.' And so saying Christian falls in a dead faint, frothing at the mouth. And when he wakes, he's on his own, with the sun setting.

That night he wriggles around, trying to make himself comfortable. In the cloister he's been in the habit of propping his body in a fixed position, with bolsters made from old ragged habits, but this is no longer feasible. Though he assumes his resting position – supine, legs apart, knees bent – it gives him no solace. The problem is, if anything, worsened by walking. The abrasions caused by the cord he uses to strap his penis to his thighs – mostly for systematic relief to his sandals, of which he has only two – are loosening the skin around the bulb. Taking his penis between his hands he studies it in the late light. The skin is definitely thinner. It's his habit to strap it first to one leg, then the other. He's tried shifting the cord higher, but in the process of walking it wears down to the bulb. As a consequence, wear is always sustained in the same area. I wonder, thinks Christian, has such a thing been seen in the reign of Boniface?

The sun goes down, and nesting birds – vultures, ravens, crows – come out of the forest beyond the field. The ditch in which Christian lies resting is a bed of partially dry mud. In the fields nearby a crop lays ruined with weeds and water. Christian lets his penis sway erect like the steeple of a church. The full moon rises, and as night wears on, Christian starts thinking of one particular woodcut.

The sun and the moon fishing for trout in peculiar streams. The stream they fish is wavy and broad, and they lay on the surface like holographs, dreamlike, floating in a heterodox way. On the near bank is a stone and a rose, on the far bank trees and a mountain.

The sun and the moon are played by men, and each man wears a diadem. The man representing the sun lays on top of the man representing the moon, and the arms of the man representing the moon go over and around the arms of the man representing the sun, so they rest at the small of that man's back, and the arms of the man representing the sun go under and around the arms of the man representing the moon, so they rest at the small of that man's back. Moreover, the legs of the man representing the moon are bent at the knees and go over and around the legs of the man representing the sun, and the legs of the man representing the sun are bent at the knees and go under and between the legs of the man representing the moon, and neither man wears a habit.

The man representing the moon is a woman.

That position, thinks Christian, who doesn't realise this, would be comfortable and soothing. But why should the sun and moon attract trout?

After a while it occurs to Christian the position he adopts himself in rest is more or less that of the man representing the moon. But the more he thinks, the more he broods, the worse his problem becomes. At midnight he starts to empty his bladder in agonising spurts of agglutinate fluid, and when he's finished the grey of dawn already fills the sky. So he gets up and walks on.

Within an hour of midday, the sun is darkened by thick black clouds. The nearest shelter is the forest. The rain starts; it advances down the road in opaque, torrential sheets. Hastily, Christian makes fast the cord to his left leg, and sets off stumbling. Back to the cloister. From the direction of the cloister he sees the laundry wagon approach.

The wagon stops and the driver, a man with whom Christian is casually acquainted, gets out. 'Take shelter' he says, and they lay down together between the sheets all fresh and clean. Suddenly it's colder, and the storm hits.

The circumcision of Christian Rosy Cross 1393.

Pulling up later outside the grogshop, the driver rushes in. 'Here, drink this' he urges, emerging with a quart pot. 'There's no more potent anaphrodisiac.'

Christian drinks till drunken. The swelling subsides, and the bleeding stops (just as well: just in time).

'Thanks mate' he says to the driver. 'How can I repay you?'
'The privilege of tending that wound' says the man, 'is recompense enough.'

They sleep the night in a rented solar. The grog wears off, and the burden returns.

'I'll show you a real good time' says the man. 'A guaranteed good time with no involvement.'

Months later, Christian decides to visit an apothecary.

'Nasty chancres on your perineum' says the apothecary. 'You've got leprosy, mate. Leprosy, from coitus with a leper, or too much conversation. A woman should expel leprous seed by dancing and/or sneezing, and you should have farted and/or ejaculated. Did you fart and/or ejaculate?'

'Never farted in my life' says Christian. 'And as for ejaculation, I've heard the word but don't know the meaning.'

'Keep watchful while sleeping. Let's take a look in the *Lilium* and *Parvus*.'

The apothecary goes to the shelf and takes down two reference works.

'Blah blah. It says here organs become the seat of ulcers after coitus at the menstrual period. The treatment, which doesn't work, consists in washing all affected parts with vinegar, water and urine, and the crusts with frictions of mercury and saliva.

'Leprosy: caused by corrupt or pestilential air, or prolonged use of melancholic foods such as lentils. Effects: nests in the brain; may break through the blood vessels causing deafness; or create maggots in the ears; or favour swelling in the nose, or fistulous ulcers about the eyes, or make the mouth a stinking hole. The voice may be paralysed. It may destroy the genitals and kidneys. Or the changes in the humours may begin in the hips and thighs, causing lack of locomotion and leg-twitch.'

'In that case, I'll be off' says Christian. 'Cheers.'

'Hold it' says the apothecary, 'this disease is notifiable. I'll have to take particulars. Where have you been living?'

'A massage parlour.'

'You mean the Dominican retreat for homeless women?'

'I guess I do.'

The apothecary puts down his books and groans.

'No wonder we find no solace. A man come in the other day and told me the world was ending. Tell you what, he had me convinced. Man with an English accent. Well son, by rights you should be living in the leper house, wearing your black cloak and hat with white patches, announcing your presence with a fair-sized rattle, and begging your one day a week .. but go on, clear out, I never saw you.'

'Thanks' says Christian, 'I'll take some leper's mercury. Am I finished? How long have I got?'

'Who knows? Apply mercury and think positively'.

'I will! Give me your biggest rattle, damn the expense!'

8

When Christian awakes in the infirmary a number of monks are standing by the bed. Among the unfamiliar faces he recognizes that of Brother Pal.

'Christian' says Pal, 'I'd like you to meet our new prior. The old one died.'

'How do you do' says the prior, a tall, scholarly man. 'Now what's the problem?'

Christian relates his problem.

'And you still have this problem?'

'I do.'

'Show it me.'

Christian does.

Christian's pain has contorted his face, so he's no longer very handsome. His hair is still black, but rather matted. His face is still pale, but very drawn. His fine tall frame has developed a cringe, and he no longer sits with his shoulders back: he slouches. He no longer cares about anything, least of all his appearance.

'How did you get this disease?' asks the prior.

'I was born with it' says Christian.

'Don't give me that, I want to *hear* about it. Do they wash themselves with salty water? Is it true they outnumber men seven to one?'

'I guess so' says Christian.

'I can well imagine a young and lustful monk with a build like yours . . . question is, are you sorry?'

'What for?'

'You know what for! Until you repent, you're wasting my time. Don't you know right from wrong?'

'No.'

'Very well; I'll be plain as I can. Don't stick this thing into other people!'

'I can't, it won't fit.'

'All right; let's talk of 'motive'.'

Christian thinks back. Desire to understand the woodcut and the *Elixir*. Ambition to own his own castle. And these are wrong?

'I can't see it, prior. I can't see wrong in what I did.'

'Very well. I'll be back shortly.'

The prior returns with a big casket emblazoned with a red cross on a white field. Argent, a cross gules. With him is Brother Pal. Christian is raving now, delirious. Complaining bitterly of ulcers.

'Drink up your lentil soup' says Pal.

'Lentils are poison to me' says Christian. 'Haven't you got any leeks?'

Pal mops the boy's brow with a putrid rag.

'There's nothing, Christian. Nothing grows. All the plants are dying out. The lentils come in on the back of a dray and we think ourselves lucky to have them. Now drink a spoonful of this soup, there's a good lad, just for me. And why don't you give that rattle a rest? You'll wear yourself out. Conserve strength.'

Christian, however, shakes his head and retains his rattle with convulsive grasp. At every shiver of his body it shakes, emitting from the bed a fierce rattle.

'Oh, now look what you've done, Christian! You've spilt the soup all over me!'

'Couldn't you heat it up or cool it down?' Twitch, rattle, shake.

'Take no notice' says the prior, sorting out his gallows chips.

Shuffle, shuffle. Pal and the prior's sandalled feet shuffle around the floor. They don't even notice. In addition, Pal is trembling with nerves, and rattling the spoon. Get rid of these slops, he thinks, tipping the remnants of the lukewarm soup into a corner of the room. An emaciated black rat hurries off at the sight of them. Pal's eyes are glazed over. Rattle, rattle. Slowly shuffling, he takes the spoon in his right hand, the plate in his left. The prior, leaving his chips unsorted, with eyes closed weaves round the bed.

Within minutes, the monastery is dancing, caught in the beat of the prophylactic rattle. The novice in the kitchen drops a sack of lentils and undulates from the room. Monks in chapel form a crocodile, working monks slap buckets and gourds. Counter-rhythms develop, resting on the pulse of Christian's rattle, which suddenly falls in abeyance.

Motion dies; everyone freezes in horrid self-awareness. The first man to break silence is the prior.

'I want this room barricaded' he shouts. 'Everyone into the chapel!'

'Why Pal' he says, as they hurry from the room, 'that was the nearest thing I ever saw. I don't like the power in that sick bay. Something diabolical in it.'

'The lentils' says Pal. 'They do you no good.'

'The way *I* see it, those evil vibes emanated from the sick bed. If ever there was a suitable case for exorcism, he is it. Maybe something in what the old prior said . . . claimed the boy possessed of demons . . . I must admit a chastening experience I found that dancing, it tested my science . . .'

'He's a sick boy, prior. Let him die in peace. He needs the comfort of his Redeemer.'

'First, I'll redeem him. I'll comfort him later.'

On the morning of his second day in isolation, Christian erupts in cankers. They are largest on his prepuce, but not inconsiderable on his nose. The prior spends most of the day watching him through a grate in the door.

'I'll attack in the morning' he says to Pal, 'at first light. See that large pox? It won't starve out you know; only way to get rid of it is through sheer terror. The boy's an unregenerate sinner, he must be affrighted into penitence. Once we get the evil humours out ...'

'Couldn't we try less drastic regimen?'

'What less drastic regimen is there? Ordinarily, I'd probably treat that large pox with mineral baths at midnight, purges, cauterizations, meals of the flesh of birds, swine and goats, tempered with spinach, fennel and asparagus – but as you know, these are troubled times Pal, and nothing grows in our accursed soil. All I have is lentils, than which, as I freely admit, it's better he should eat nothing. But what can I do? In any event, illness springs from the spirit, and spreads to the mind and body. Darkness is not of mind or body, but spirit. Don't trifle with symptoms; I learnt that at the *Studium*. We'll use what we have on hand – corpses, coffin nails, gallows chips, holy water – that way we'll get to the seat of the canker. Thirty years too late for Black Death, but well in time for Armageddon.'

On the morning of the third day, Christian's door is flung open as the first glow of morning appears, and the prior, Pal and two friars enter. The friars are dragging a scorbutic corpse, and the prior has his casket under one arm, and is carrying a bottle of holy water. Pal is bearing an old church bell.

'Now' says the prior, 'drop this attitude or perish! Look at this' – he grabs Christian's head and directs it at the corpse – 'and this!' – he opens the casket and holds up before Christian's astonished face an assortment of gallows chips – 'and this' – he takes from the casket a lurid painting depicting Hell – 'and what's your reaction?'

Christian can't think of one. Weakly, he looks at Pal, who looks away.

The friars set the corpse up on a chair next to the bed, and the prior instructs Pal to stand by with holy water. Pouring it out over Christian's body the prior intones, 'I pour you out in the name of our Lord Jesus Christ born in Bethlehem.' Then pouring it over Christian's face he intones, 'I pour this over you in the name of our Lord Jesus Christ tortured in Jerusalem.' Then he takes an amulet of coffin nails, and hangs it on Christian.

The prior conducts a full exorcism. By the time he's finished it's close on midday, and Christian is soaked with holy water, weak from scourging, deaf from abuse, and practically insensible. He feels no better, even so.

'Well that's it', says the prior. 'You'll heal up now; but if there's no improvement by tonight, I'll take the remainder of our stock of dried herbs, work it into a clear paste, say seven masses over the preparation while adding garlic and holy water, and you'll drink the mixture for supper from the church bell. And if you're no better in the morning, it's off to the leprosarium, because if there's one thing I can't tolerate, it's an obdurate sinner.'

Seizing the casket he strides from the room. Pal walks over to Christian's bed and kneels. The corpse sits propped up grinning.

'Christian' moans Pal. 'Don't despair. I know the prior's methods won't work, but he's not a cruel man, just stupid.'

'Don't say that' croaks Christian. 'He speaks highly of you.'

Christian's condition is not improved by ingestion of herbal nostra; the prior's disgusted.

'I'm disgusted' he says to Pal, as they peer through the grate at the sleeping boy, rattle in hand, and by this stage practically the same colour as the cadaver. 'The treatment didn't work. By rights, I ought to torture him as a contumacious felon. But you know, Pal, when I see that boy's condition, with all those suppurating cankers, it makes me glad I'm not the lustful type.'

'You're not going to torture him.'

'I can't be bothered. If I set out to torture every miserable creature I came across I'd have no time for anything else. Besides, I've lost interest in the case. I'll send him off to the leprosarium. My feeling is he won't last long.'

'In that case' says Pal, 'you have no objection to my consoling the boy?'

'Feel free, Pal. But do it in your own time. I notice sheets in abundance.'

'And absolutely filthy' says Pal. 'I've been meaning to complain.'

'Oh? To whom?'

'That's what I wanted to ask. Where do they come from? Where do they go?'

'I always thought that was your department. The retreat I guess; why ask?'

'It's their condition, prior. I shouldn't have thought that homeless women . . .'

'Come on Pal! We're grown men. The succubus and incubus are everywhere. Wholesale destruction impends. It's a rare night the succubus doesn't visit me, but I take preventative measures.'

'Oh?'

'Plates of holy water round the bed.'

'And does it work?'

'No, but the thought's there. I do what I can, I can do no more. It's not as though I'm being punished with cankers, now is it? Be honest. Were that the case, rest assured I'd take more drastic action.'

Pal spends the week with Christian. On Christian's insistence they use up all the mercury treating Christian's crusts, but the crusts remain, and Christian is now coal-black as well as half dead, head to toe.

'Ah Christian' murmurs Pal. 'At least you won't want for cerements.'

'How's that?' croaks Christian, toad-like.

'Just talking to myself' says Pal. 'Took you to be sleeping.'

'Something about sheets' croaks Christian.

'They're very dirty, that's all.'

'You know where those sheets come from Pal? A massage parlour. I meant to tell you.'

'You're delirious, Christian.'

'Think about it, Pal. See if it doesn't make sense.'

He's in the final stage, thinks Pal. The blood's come back to the white patches on his black face.

'Well?'

'Of course it makes sense Christian, excellent sense.'

'Don't humour me Pal, you've wasted your life! Get out you fool, get out now!'

'I'm not allowed out, you know that.'

Christian leans over and grabs Pal's scapula.

'Have I ever lied, to your knowledge?'

'Not to my knowledge, Christian.'

'Then join me in an expedition! We'll go to the Holy Land! You're entitled to an expiatory pilgrimage, and I can bathe in the River Jordan, like Naaman the Syrian leper!'

'Christian. For you, I'll do it.'

'No you won't do it' says the prior. 'I need you here to wash sheets. Besides, man, Christian won't last to the first bend of the road. Look at him! You must be out of your mind. His rattle has practically grafted.'

'It's better than dying in a leper house.'

'Such pilgrims! An old man and a leprous brat. Infidels, beware! Take care, Saracens! You won't get out of Germany Pal, but that's your affair.'

'My information, sir, is the nunnery is a whorehouse!'

'Don't say such things, Pal. What you must remember, those women are not nuns, but hark! Impassioned knocking!'

A friar irrupts with a ghastly expression.

'Prior' he says, 'there's been a terrible accident by the main gate! The laundry cart has tipped over spilling the sheets in the mud, and the driver is dead.'

'Well how do you like that?' says the prior. 'I was going to get him to take Christian to the leprosarium this morning. Maybe God smiles on your enterprise Pal, let's hope so. Can you see any point in it?'

'I certainly can' says Pal. 'That which is extrinsic and corruptible must be separated from that which is intrinsic and incorruptible.'

'I'll say this' says the prior, 'you've a nice turn of phrase for a man who's spent a lifetime in the laundry.'

9

Having heard mass, the two companions set out. In addition to clothes and a copy of the gospels, they take an *Old Compendium* to help them find their way, some coffin nails for Christian and a dog to guard the horse. By midday they're many miles from the cloister, deep in the forbidding forest. The horse plods on, straining to drag the cart over ruts and corrugations. The dog sleeps. Christian complains unceasingly, shifting his body this way and that. He kneels backwards, for the best view. Pal drives, with the reins in his hands and a far-off expression on his senile face, as though he can see the Holy Sepulchre itself, dead centre of the *oikoumene*.

At midday they pull over in a small clearing and munch a few lentils.

'Are you sure we're going the right way Pal?'

'I think so, Christian. Left at the gate, then follow the road till you come to the limits of the empire. Then cross the Alps, arriving at the seaport of Venice. Then catch a boat.'

'How long will it take?'

Pal gets up and removes a loose-leaf map from the compendium.

'Here we are. Look Christian. Up here at the top in the east, we have Asia. Underneath Asia, Europe. Separating Africa from Asia is a river called the Nile, and separating Europe from Africa, *Mare Nostrum*, in which floats an island called Balaeres. Paradise is to the east.'

'But this map is 300 years old!'

'Some things never change, son. We're at present *en route* for Asia, so have to cross the sea. I hear the best time to cross the Alps is August. But the best time to sail is April.'

'Why is this forest not on the map? Are you sure we're not

heading north? It seems to be getting colder.'

'Ah – that's because we're climbing. Mountains are cold in their own right. The dense lower air is heated, but the cool upper air is not. Think of it this way; in summer the birds of prey fly high in the air to cool off. Learn from Nature. That which is hot and dry must be placed above that which is cold and wet.'

'All right. Why are those men approaching now coming from below us?'

'That's because they're on the ground, and we're in this cart. It's also because the warm, dense, lower air plays tricks on the eyes the upper air does not. At the level of Olympus, illusion vanishes.'

As the men draw near, the dog starts barking and Christian rattles his rattle. A little while later, the men are in the cart, and our two companions on the ground. The cart, with the men in it, disappears towards the cloister.

'Now how did that happen?' asks Christian. 'Why did you let those men take our cart?'

'You heard them, Christian. They had us over a barrel. They asked if we were mendicants, and when I said we were, they asked if we owned the cart. Now of course, as everyone knows, a mendicant can't own anything.'

'I'm sorry, Paul, but you're going to have to carry me.'

Suffice it to say, they make it to Venice. It so happens on their first day there, they're attracted by a large crowd. Before long, our friends are standing in the front rank, with a whole file to themselves. The preacher, haranguing the crowd in Italian, glances at the pilgrims with scarcely a pause, but his audience is more interested. This is partly because Christian is carrying Pal – Pal is by this stage crippled – and partly because Christian is either harbouring a concealed weapon, or setting a new style in the codpiece. He's fixed a ram's horn under his habit during the Alpine crossing, fully two feet long, with a pronounced upward sweep where the end's broken off. Hollow inside, it raises the hem of his tattered habit to close on knee level.

Pal, though he doesn't understand a word, is so impressed by the speaker, he asks Christian to move in close.

At this, the mob erupts.

'Assassins!'

'That was most embarrassing' says Christian.

'I know' says John, the preacher. 'I understand. But surely it's better to be stripped naked than beaten to a pulp? And what about those invitations out?'

'They all wish they had his build' says Pal. 'I've told him before.'

'I'm going nowhere' says Christian, sulking. 'Not after they smashed my ram's horn.'

'Ah yes, but once the excitement wears off, you'll have no *need* of it!'

Pal moves over. 'That's the problem. Christian lives in anticipation.'

'Good Lord' says the friar. 'This is Christian Rosencreutz.'

'Of course' says Pal. 'There could only be the one.'

One day, shortly after Christmas, a friar called Anselm appears in the yard and says to Christian, 'Haven't you anything better to do than mope about all day?'

'Mind your own business' says Christian.

'I've heard of your rudeness' says the friar, 'but I've also heard of your physique. Fix a pair of wings to those ankles, I'd show you how to make a small fortune. Would you care to make a small fortune?'

'I don't know about a *small* one' says Christian, 'but the only way of making a *large* fortune that appeals to me is by chemistry.'

'You need to have faith in that' says Anselm, 'and have your failures made you wise?'

'There are certain things I won't try again' says Christian, 'but that leaves plenty.'

'Come with me, Christian. I've something to show you.'

'Now wait a minute friend, I've been caught before. What do you know of the *Prima Materia*?'

'I actually saw it, at a friend's house. I was sceptical myself, till I witnessed the *transformation*. The adept was a converted Jew, I never knew his name. He kept the *Stone* in a phial, and all he would say was that it is a viscous water found everywhere, which if openly named would revolutionize the world. Of course we don't want that, at this stage. When further pressed, he described it as dark, disesteemed and grey. I asked him how much it would cost, and he said nothing, apart from time and maintenance. The work is easy, the act is simple. A boy of sixteen could do it.'

'Now that's interesting' says Christian. 'The last description *I* heard, was of a subtle earth, brown and opaque.'

'Well that's philosophy for you. I've read every book on the subject, and on one point only, philosophers agree. The name of the *Stone* is forever hidden, without divine illumination.'

'That's no good to me' explains Christian. 'I want instant gratification.'

'Wait – there is another way. Sages who've received the Secret occasionally communicate their knowledge to pupils under a pledge of inviolable secrecy. That is, a pledge to convert the world, through gibberish.'

'I won't tell a soul' says Christian.

'Wouldn't matter if you did' says Anselm. 'Come with me, I've a book you should see.'

'Hmm' says Christian, 'how much did *this* cost?' The book is very ancient.

'Nothing' says Anselm, 'what do you think?'

The cover is gold, with a big indentation, and graven with strange letters.

'I don't think much of the cover.'

'Never judge a book by its cover, Christian. Not unless the author designed the jacket.'

Within are twenty-one leaves, all covered in the same strange letters and here and there painted figures. These consist, on the frontispiece, of a virgin; serpents swallowing her up; a serpent crucified; a desert or wilderness containing a large number of fountains, whence issue serpents here and there; within, a young man with a caducean rod writhen about by two serpents; against him running and flying with open wings an old man with an hour glass on his head and a scythe in his hand; a flower coloured red and white, much shaken by the north wind on the top of a high mountain around the base of which sleep griffins and dragons; a rose tree, growing up against a hollow oak from the foot of which bubbles a fountain of pure white water which many who dig in the earth seek, but few can find; a king with a falchion slaying infants, their mothers standing by forlorn; these infants' blood being gathered by soldiers, who put it in a vessel, wherein Sol and Luna bathe.

'What do you make of it?' asks Christian.

'I can only assume this is the book with which Rhases was pummelled by the Khorassan Emir. You'll note the dent in the cover is the size of a man's head, assuming he wore a fair-sized turban. It was the death of poor Rhases. He should have stayed in Baghdad. I showed a page to an Arab merchant, and he said it was written in cipher. I haven't deciphered the cipher as yet. The Emir of Khorassan is said to have paid Rhases one thousand pieces of gold for this book.'

'Then why'd he hit him over the head with it?'

'Can't you guess? The very act of hitting an old man with a book betrays him. Could you imagine a brutal man completing the *Magisterium*?'

'Sure. As long as he followed instructions.'

'You don't know much about chemistry. Perhaps I'd better explain.'

Anselm starts pacing up and down.

'According to Aristotle, there are four noble sciences; chemistry, physics, magic and astrology. Of these, chemistry must be studied for its own sake. Anyone who studies it for other than its own sake will end up with nothing but vexation, for the sages deliberately present this science in the most perplexing cant they can. In fact, our Art is more noble and precious than any other, with the sole exception of the doctrine of the Glorious Redemption, through our Lord Jesus Christ. God reveals this Art to His elect, and it's the duty of His elect to obfuscate. Rest assured of one thing, Christian, this book is for the Sons of the Doctrine, for if the hidden Stone, which is the gift of God, does not mingle with Our Stone, a man ends up with a nasty black tar no matter how hard he tries.'

'Oh well' says Christian, 'perhaps I can help. God just cured me of a serious disease.'

'I don't know – you don't strike me as God-fearing.'

'Come on Anselm, an *Arab* wrote that book. What would a greasy Arab know?'

'It is a fact, Christian, the Stone exalts the heathen. Rhases describes the Resurrection and the Trinity.'

'Very well. I can only offer.'

After a week of sitting in the yard and dwelling on the imagery, Christian approaches Anselm and asks, 'What would be the most abhorrent thing a monk could do?'

'Break his vows I guess. So what's the verdict on the gilded book?'

'I'll make you an offer – twice what you paid. I like the illustrations.'

'Give it away? That's the worst thing I can think of!'

'All right, at least tell me where you got it.'

'I'll give you a clue. The place is crawling with philosophers and chemists, because of the rose bushes and snakes, and the statue of the Sun God that stood in ancient times at the entrance to the harbour there. It was so big a full-rigged ship could sail between its legs.'

10

Christian heads for Rhodes, leaving Pal behind on Cyprus. In the old town he takes refuge in the doorway of a house he fancies. He's heard that on Rhodes sages go round dressed like anyone else.

For himself, he's wearing an old burnous, picked up cheap from a palmer on the docks. He bears a moneybag and carries a staff.

O Sons of the Rumour and Investigators of the Wisdom of the Whole Wide World: is this not the Isle where Pallas was born while Gold Rain fell?

Eventually the door opens, affording Christian a chance to impress.

'My first is in sun but not in moon; my second in runt but not in rune; my third in four but not in five; when I am dead I am still alive; my fourth is in nay but never in yea; my fifth precisely the other way; and I must seven times begin before I may be clean of sin. What am I?'

'Whatever you are' says the man at the door, 'you're wasting my time. Stand back.'

He shakes a big black mat.

'Furnace dust' says Christian. 'I recognize it well.'

'I don't need an assistant. Now, if you'll excuse me . . .'

Christian flashes his trump card; the gilded book.

'All right' says the man, 'you win. Chance favours the prepared mind and you found me, I didn't find you.'

He shuts the great oak door, and at once the sound of the sea and the heat of the day are locked out, and there is silence.

'My lab's upstairs' says the man. 'Bernard's the name. So you got in the door, congratulations. Now for some bad news: my tincture's gone. I used it up, every grain. In fact I'm heavily in debt. I appeal to your good senses; would I live here if I had the tincture? Now, what book is that?'

'The Light of Lights' says Christian, repeating what Anselm has said.

'I'd take *that* with a grain of mercuric sulphide if I were you. Where'd you get it?'

'I'm sorry, I can't divulge my sources.'

'I see ... stolen ... but this is remarkable ... extraordinary ... clarity of the plates ... clarity of the text ... undoubtedly authentic ... and on my own doorstep. Is someone trying to tell me something?'

'Someone told *me* this was The Light of Lights, by Rhases.'

'No, I have a facsimile edition, and this is not it. Amazing. There was a time I'd have offered 100,000 denars for this volume.'

'I would have sold it, too' says Christian. 'But now I know it must be worth several times that much.'

Bernard laughs.

'What have you heard about me?'

'Nothing' says Christian. 'I slept in the doorway because I fancy the house.'

'You mean you don't know who I am?'

'How could I? I came to Rhodes in search of an adept, but didn't know where to find one. I'm a Son of the Doctrine.'

'Are you. And what's your name?'

'Christian Rosy Cross.'

Bernard rises and paces about the room in agitation.

'Many years back I came into possession of a large quantity of the Red Tincture. Like you, I was an avid seeker after wisdom and wealth. Through a remarkable experience, I came into possession of the Stone, which made me, in potential at least, the wealthiest man in the world. I didn't prepare the tincture; it was given my by an artist. He came literally to my doorstep, in much the same way as you, round midnight. I was inside poring over spagyric texts. I opened the door, and found this old, ragged man. When he professed himself an adept, I smiled. Not unnaturally, I reasoned a man who possessed the secret of wealth would not dress in rags and wander the streets like a vagabond. He saw my smile, and I still remember the words he spoke to me: "Son" he said, "God has granted me a great gift, of which the making of gold is a diversion. I have only recently arrived at a full understanding, because the world is full of wickedness that obscures a man's mind from the nature of true wealth. I am old and sprightly: I wish to dispose of my elixir, no longer have any need for it; but I daren't flush it down the drain for fear it will convert the plumbing of this city. Accordingly, I have left it standing in your doorway. I know from your reputation and see from your books you have a lively and inquiring mind. So I will teach you briefly, and by an oblique procedure, what it's taken me a lifetime to learn: the nature of true wealth. When I have gone, do with my tincture as you wish. Take it up if you dare. Keep it if you are not ready. Dispose of it if you are wise. For if God has elected you to His Fraternity, He will provide you with all you need."

'With this enigmatic remark, he walked off. I thought he couldn't have been serious. I was beginning to doubt the existence of the tincture. But after he'd gone, I found he had indeed left a phial of red powder, and I took it in. I set to work, and within an hour, found it was as he had said – the Red Tincture of the Philosophers! Moreover, of sufficient virtue to convert one hundred thousand times its weight to purest virgin gold.

'Now we come to the surprising part. Would you credit, from that day on, I have not had a moment's peace of mind? Consider my situation; a man well known as a seeker after Knowledge, suddenly comes into possession of it. Would it not arouse immediate suspicion if he made a great show of his wealth? The news would spread like wildfire, and the greed for gold, as we both know, being the strongest passion known to man, he might well fear for his safety.

'On the pretext of travelling to foreign parts in search of a master, I went to Paris, where, disguised as a Cossack, I took some gold I had made by projection to the goldsmith's shop.

The goldsmith took one look at it and said, this gold was made by Art. I asked him how he knew. Because of its purity, he said: this is purer gold than ever came from a mine. Hearing this, I ran off, and never returned for my gold or the money. Even so, several roughnecks followed me, and it was only by fleeing I escaped. You may not know it, but the possession of chemical gold is a criminal offence. What is more, transmission of gold across state borders is strictly governed. Anyone who seems to have more than he should is certain to be charged with smuggling. The result? Though I possessed great wealth, I could not use it. I lived in constant fear of being set upon by villains. I began to waste my tincture, projecting it onto all sorts of trashy amalgams, in order to see if I could not make gold less pure. I essayed my tincture onto copper, iron, brass, pewter, tin glass, spelter, solder, regulus – but always the same thing happened: my medicine conquered all imperfection, and turned everything to purest gold! And because I had the tincture, but not the mercury, I had no means of multiplying my stone.

'I won't bore you with details, but I lived in utter misery. I dared not sell a grain of gold, for fear of exciting suspicion. I couldn't take a wife or friend, but moved continually from town to town. In the end, I grew reckless, and used up all my tincture making a medicine called "Leper's Mercury", which I sold to a German apothecary. Then, on learning a certain count had a house on Rhodes he wished to sell, I took the last of my virgin gold and paid his price.

'A week later, soldiers came to my room and dragged me off. "It's evident you made this gold by Art" said the greedy count. "I'll provide you with all you need, if you'll make me more. It's wartime."

'In vain I protested I had no tincture, and couldn't make more. He wouldn't believe me. Threatened with torture and death, I laboured for many years, with nothing to show at the end of that time but the invention of fairy floss. Eventually I sent word to the count that he might as well kill me. Instead, he sent me here, and now you appear, with the book M.'

'The book M?'

'The book M.'

'I never heard of it.'

'Few have. Apparently, it was written by John on Patmos, not far from here. Now John, as you're probably aware, was an adept, imprisoned on Patmos by a tyrant. While on Patmos he wrote two chemical texts, the Book of Revelation and M. M is the less obscure, and describes the synthesis of the New Jerusalem – the purification of earth through Art – hinted at in Revelation. I don't know how you came to get your hands on this book. I don't care. But I think we should accept the challenge. You provide the book, I'll provide the know-how.'

'Great' says Christian. The tincture exists! I can hardly believe my good fortune.'

'Neither can I' says Bernard.

No expense has been spared with the lab, but what impresses Christian most is the Baphometic figure on the mantelpiece.

'Who's that man with the goat's head Bernard? A philosopher?'

'You will note one hand points down, Christian, signifying the Stone is conceived in the retort, and one hand points up, signifying the Stone is born in the helmet. That is, the stinking water, smelling of sulphur and the grave, must be driven to the helmet, till its evil stench turns into a sweet quintessence, which, as Lullius says, is enough to stand a bird still in its flight. The horns and wings signify the matter must rise; the cloven hooves and hairy arse it must sink again, having risen. Yes, anything that turns the mind towards chemistry is welcome in my laboratory; the problem is, deciding what to keep out.'

'How do you mean?'

'Well, after a few years at the bench, everything takes on chemical meaning. The mind, victim of an *idée fixe* and demented through overwork, starts to see everything in hermetic terms. It's not uncommon for a chemist to suffer delusions of mantic grandeur, in which he surveys the macrocosm as though from the right-hand side of God. Such a man eventually retires from the lab and moves into the study, where he sets about composing a lucubration that allows of as many interpretations as there are literates in the *oikoumene*. Such are the majority of chemical works, but the book M was written when practice kept pace with theory."

'Then you don't think . . .'

'I never think, Christian. It's fatal to the bench chemist. I've seen it happen too many times. No, perseverance is the answer; speculation solves nothing. Any fool can speculate, but making the Tincture demands Art. I don't deny the Resurrection, but see this retort in my hand? It is a retort. It is not the soul of man. It is not the womb of the Virgin Mother. It is not the belly of the Microprosopus. It's a retort, and nothing else. You see, when the ancient chemists decided to conceal their nomenclature, the favorite and natural butt for their spleen were their bitter antagonists, the mystics. Out of context, it's almost impossible for us to understand their satire. What was meant as parody is often taken for the Real Thing, and vice versa. That strike you as paradoxical?'

'Yes and no' says Christian.

'Why don't we make our own lead, Bernard?'

'We can't make base metals Christian; we don't know their composition. We can only make gold, which has no impure sulphur, by means of our Stone, which is pure quicksilver. Basically, that which is volatile and flees the fire, like a dove, is called soul; that which remains in the fire, like a salamander, is called body; and that which unites body and soul is called mercury, or spirit. Now if the soul remains with the body, we have success. But what generally happens is the soul rises taking the body with it. To watch the furnace closely is the whole secret of the Art. Nature, alone, cannot effect the desired union of body and soul which is brought about by our Stone; there is no one to take the vessel from the heat.

'Basically speaking, the artist watches for the proper moment, and after the conjunction, fears nothing more from the fire: it's in all the books. When conjunction takes place, brought about by a well-tempered fire, the action of which is stopped by the watchful, many remarkable phenomena occur. Afterwards the artist rests, and what follows, as Socrates says, is nothing but woman's work and child's play. The critical part is in knowing when to commence the fermentation; this should be done precisely when the Stone is germinating. After all, as Rhases says, what a man sows, that shall he reap. However, I cannot stress too strongly the secret is in the fire: if the heat is taken beyond a certain point, that which has been generated is ruined, and the Magisterium destroyed. Nature always goes beyond the proper point, but man's will is free.

'We'll use the book M. In fact going by that book, I don't see how we can fail.'

They fail. 'I can't understand it' says Bernard. 'Less than a lunar month, record time. We'll have to go over the entire experiment to the point of that explosion. Got your notebooks handy?'

'Right. We took the young man with wings at his ankles and, striking his helmet with a caducean rod, cleansed him with vinegar and salt, sublimed him, coagulated him, and dissolved him in an equal quantity of common salt. We pounded him in a brass mortar, placed him in a glazed pot, poured on his head four times as much vinegar again, and left him over a gentle fire till the vinegar had all dissolved. We removed him from the fire, placed him in a dish, and washed him with pure water to rinse out the salt. We took the same quantity of green leonine atrament, freshly prepared from ultramontane atrament by heating in a sealed jar over coals and kept till use under urine, and allowed the green lion to devour the white flower of the mountainous plant by pounding the two together, placing them in an aludel, and making a paste of them with pure water. We dried the mixture over a gentle flame and carefully stopped up the mouth of our vessel with clay of sages. The vessel was left on a slow fire from morn till night with the fire increasing. On cooling and opening the vessel, we expected to find our old man with his scythe would have cut the wings off the feet of our young man with his helmet, but instead of a substance snow-white in appearance and reconciled like camphor, we found a tatty grey residuum, disposed to fly in our eyes. Nonetheless, we pounded this, poured on it a twofold quantity of water of atrament, and left the mixture for eight days. During this time we expected that red flowers would grow on our rose bush, and our dragons and griffins fall asleep. And indeed, it appeared so. We skimmed off what floated on the surface, coagulated it, and kept it dust-free. It was not as red as it should have been.

'In the meantime, we took 3 ounces of olive oil in a glazed pot, boiled it over a slow fire, threw in one-sixth the amount of yellow flowers of sulphur, shook the whole, removed it from fire after the flowers had dissolved in the dew, and added one ounce of our coagulate. We sublimed this over a fierce fire, whereupon our vessel exploded. Interpreting this as the king slaying the innocent with his falchion, you gathered up the blood while I stood by and wept.

'Taking our blood, we put it in an open vessel, adding Sol and Luna in due course. We then took our plant with its gold and silver leaves, and sought to corrupt it into serpents, which, being crucified and dried, would give us that which we desired. However, our plant defied corruption. It yielded up on heating its gold and silver, signifying the bird had flown.

'Now to my mind, there can only be one explanation. Our young man was poisoned; that is, our mercury contained arsenic. There remains one hope. I know of a shop in Damascus where they sell the world's purest mercury, arsenic-free. It comes from a mine in India. I believe Arab adepts use none other. Of course, I'd love to go myself, but I daren't leave this house.'

'Now wait a minute, Bernard. You're not sending me to the land of the Infidel!'

'Listen Christian, you want the Work to work or not? You look more like a Saracen than Saladin himself in that getup, and I'm sure you'll pick up the lingo in no time. Get down to the docks, there's a good boy, and find out when the next boat's leaving.'

11

Rhodes is a stone's throw from the mainland, but the overland route is impractical. Christian boards a small felucca stinking of olive oil. When the movement of the boat allows it, he takes coin from his moneybag and spins it in the air. Hard cash. What a lustre, against the blue of the sea. And soon there'll be plenty more, enough to buy Christian his castle.

Bernard has told him that he who possesses the Mastery has nothing to fear from travel. Adepts, whether Latin or Arab, take no interest in formal religion, realizing that Christendom and Islam have much in common, worse luck.

On the third day out of Rhodes, with the weather fine and a stiff breeze blowing, Christian is disturbed from his reverie of castles by a racket amidships. Several of the crew are shouting and pointing at a large vessel approaching from the north, lateen-rigged, and riding low in the water. On seeing it, the captain gives orders for the crew to run the ship before the wind. At this, Christian stumbles from his coign, and asks why course has been altered.

'Pirates' snaps an elderly Jew. 'Don't you know a privateer when you see one?'

'What do they want from us?' asks an Arab. 'We carry nothing of value.'

The pirates come alongside and grapple the ships together. They're a scurvy looking crowd, well armed. Their leader, a man of horrendous appearance wearing a red turban, comes quietly on deck and confers with the merchant captain in the prow of the felucca.

After a few minute's talk, the captain returns with a relieved expression and says, 'I'm advised we're in no danger. They're looking for the most beautiful boy in the Levant, rumoured to be on board. I can't see it' – the Jews laugh and so do the pirates – 'but I'll have to ask you to take off your clothes.'

Christian hurriedly sheds his burnous. The sooner they get this over, the better. Of course, they'll see he's no Saracen, but that can't be helped.

At a nod from the leader, two pirates step forward and Christian is seized by the arms.

'Hey' he shouts, 'What about the rest of them! They haven't got their clothes off yet!'

'Nice and gentle' says the pirate leader. 'He's worth a lot of money. The Sultan of Damcar has offered 100,000 denars for his capture.'

'There must be some mistake' says Christian.

'There's no mistake' says a Jew.

'You're a fine style of boy' says the pirate leader. 'The Sultan will care for you well. I understand he wants you for his personal catamite.'

'I've business to attend to' protests Christian. 'I'm a businessman!'

Despite his pleas, he's taken away, no one lifting a finger to prevent it.

'Don't cry' say the pirates, devout Moslems all. 'You get the chance to save your soul, whatever happens to your body.'

But Christian's not worried about his body, he's used to the inconvenience. With the aid of his staff he can walk fairly well.

But what hope for the Work now? And just as things were going so *well*!

*S*on of Christian Rosy Cross

Resumé

'... *To such an intention of a general reformation, the most godly and highly-illuminated Father, our Brother, CRC, a German, the chief and original of our Fraternity, hath much and long time laboured, who, by reason of his poverty (although descended of noble parents), in the fifth year of his age was placed in a cloyster, where he had learned indifferently the Greek and Latin tongues, and (upon his earnest desire and request), being yet in his growing years, was associated to a Brother, PAL, who had determined to go to the Holy Land. Although his brother dyed in Ciprus, and so never came to Jerusalem, yet our Brother CRC did not return, but shipped himself over . . .* '

Fama Fraternitatis

12

Christian arrives at the Syrian capital Damascus some days later; he's managed to escape.

Damascus, in 1394, is the world's most beautiful city. It lies at the foot of a mountain range, in the midst of a river plain watered by mountain springs, melting snow and liquified rock. The plain is covered in vegetable gardens of lettuce and asparagus, flower gardens of lilies, violets and roses, and orchards of dates, plums, apples, mulberries, figs and pomegranates. There's also wheat.

Larger than Paris, Damascus enjoys great stability under its sultans, with a population such that the city spreads beyond the city walls. There are plenty of fashionable suburbs and country estates.

The mountains to the west of the city are high and beautiful certainly, but not as high and beautiful as the Caucausus to the north. The Caucausus are so high and beautiful that Circassians, according to Aristotle, enjoy two-thirds as much sunlight again as everybody else.

Lapis projectus est in terras, & in montibus exaltatus, & in aere habitat, & in flumine pascitur, id est, Mercurius.

Christian enters the city gate on the back of an ass. One minute there he is, standing next to a forge in the suburbs, manacled with a moneybag of gold, the next he's free, riding an ass, and penniless.

Never mind, he thinks; in a place like this I can always find a week's work in a laundry.

Just inside the gate his ass drops dead. Christian surveys it ruefully. What appears to be a coloured dye of some sort is running down its nose.

The next morning Christian wakes in a ward of the local hospital. Infectious disease is the scourge of monastic life (as above, so below: the enlightened mind operates from the collapsed immune system – anyone for unilateral disarmament?) A doctor and a group of medical students stand by the bed.

'Come a long way?' asks the doctor, in fluent German.

Christian says nothing.

'Interesting case' continues the doctor. 'Frankish.' He lifts the sheet. 'Dehydration and heatstroke, but take a look at this: satyriasis. Any ideas?'

With all that fresh fruit to eat, Christian recovers in no time. 'When will they let me out?' he asks his neighbour in the next bed. 'I'm here on business.'

'What's your hurry?' says the man. 'Lay back and enjoy. The Mongols are coming.'

'That's all right for *you*' says Christian, 'I can't afford the treatment.' He refers to a leather harness.

'It's free and gratis' says the man. 'This is the curio ward. I can't move my neck since kissing the Kaaba, and they tell me it's all in the mind.'

The next morning Christian, discharged, is sitting outside the Piebald Palace, his favorite building, wondering whether to get a job or go on traveller relief, when a group of Franks walks by. Among them is Brother Anselm.

That does it, thinks Christian. The more reason to hurry back to Rhodes!

There are synagogues, Christian churches, pagan temples and opulent mosques; wine shops and brothels, carpet shops, silver shops, gold shops, but no chemist's supplies. There are shops that sell spices and shops that sell scent, men who wear skullcaps and men who wear fur hats, black men, white men, orientals, soldiers and priests galore. There are sword shops, belt shops, saddle shops, cake shops, shops of every kind, it seems, but the one Christian seeks.

Fed up, he stands outside the mosque, waiting his turn for the boiled sweets that someone leaves for the poor in a wooden trough: you need to be early. While eating his sweets, he sits in a vine-trellised rosegarden, watching the throng. In the centre of this garden is a golden fountain featuring a marble bird tearing its breast. It looks beautiful with the sun on it.

It has to be here somewhere, thinks Christian, but what do I do for money? He feels through the folds of his laundered burnous to see if he can find a dirhem, but all he can find is a dirty old lump of shit, from the hospital laundry. He picks it out and chucks it in a rosebush.

At once, a passing soldier wearing a beaver cloak and red satin surtout, dismounts and walks over.

'Did I see you littering?' he says. 'Pick it up!'

Sighing, Christian complies. As he searches, a stiff kick from the soldier's boot sends him sprawling.

What a prick, thinks Christian, bleeding from a thorn in the mouth. He put the shit back in his cloak and leaves the garden. Seeing a passing newsboy, he asks for a late Latin edition.

There's a vacancy for a masseur.

'You were lucky' says the newsboy. 'That emir has a reputation for halving boys at the waist. By the will of Allah, his sword got stuck in his scabbard. Very holy!'

'My change' says Christian. 'I gave you a denar.' When your luck's in, you may as well push it.

13

Despite his inexperience Christian lands the job, largely on account of his physique.

The massage parlour, at the back of a bazaar in a lane near the viceroy's palace, caters mainly for soldiers, who stiffen up in the barracks. Known locally as 'Turks', they range in age from younger than Christian to older than Pal, and include Griffins, as well as Kipchaks, Franks and Mongols. Circassians mainly, big, rough, bandy fellows.

'Why are there no Arab soldiers?' Christian inquires.

This brings the house down in the foyer, where clients sit sipping sherbet. It turns out Arabs can't fight.

'Then what *are* they good for?' asks Christian.

'That's a good question' says Christian's main patron, the Sugar Turk, an emir of ten whose jacket pockets are always filled with sugar. He doesn't live in the barracks; he owns barracks himself. 'They're useless cunts, a bunch o' big shielas. Know what I mean?'

The girl on his lap leaps and shrieks, the Sugar Turk jumps and runs. Christian gives chase, all part of the job. His clients are mainly guilty old men, some of them local merchants. Christian's speciality is ethical massage. Brandishing a rose switch, he forces the client to confess his sins, then thrashes him. Got the idea from a Franciscan prior.

'Christian's a virgin' confirms the madam. 'You look, but you mustn't touch. What makes you think your evil paws and jaws are up to the job?'

The girls sneer, why wouldn't they; you should see *their* clothing. Christian, by contrast, when he goes out, wears only his old black burnous. 'He's pious' confirms the madam, 'dresses frugal, and only goes out for knowledge. He's an intellectual. What he looks for, he can't find.'

I'll give it another week, thinks Christian, but looks like Bernard was mistaken.

On the afternoon of the day before he intends leaving Damascus, Christian is freshening up his rose switch waiting for his next client, when he hears the door to the parlour being opened and shut without permission.

'Haven't I seen you before?' he inquires. The man at the door is The One.

Properly speaking, The Two.

'You may have dreamt of me' says The One. He starts moving his hands in a strange pattern, indicating he would like Christian to do the same.

It's pretty hard not to. Moving his hands in a clumsy circle, Christian feels greatly relieved. 'I've been here before' he tells The One. 'Years back, I remember now. The place is familiar to me. You ride a black horse, am I right?'

The One smiles. He never shuts his eyes. He never even blinks. He takes out a small set of scales and puts them on the massage bench. Then he takes out a small bottle of red powder and places it in the scales.

'A measure of wheat for a penny' he says, 'and three measures of barley for a denar. Now counterweigh this.'

Well Christian tries everything. In the end he presses his whole weight on the vacant pan. Nothing happens.

The One removes the bottle and tosses it in the air. It seems to hover. It weighs less than a feather, when held in the hand.

'We await you in Damcar' says The One.

'I know' says Christian. 'But where *is* Damcar? No one ever heard of it!'

'As near as the sweat on your brow' says The One, 'as far as the sun in your sky.' He places the bottle on the bench, then palms it and holds it up.

'The difference between those two bottles' he says, 'is most instructive.'

'Do you await me in Damcar' says Christian. 'Do you sell pure mercury there?'

'No, but we give away the Stone.'

'I tell you what, I might call in and collect some. Can you give me directions? And what about cost? I hear they've devalued the currency.'

'Put not faith in filthy gold' says The One, 'but search your garment. Cheers.'

He smiles, points at the ceiling with two erect fingers, then disappears.

'Hey Christian' says a voice at the door, 'are you okay?'

'Sure' says Christian. 'By the way, who was that?'

'We don't know. But he came through the door and it was shut at the time.'

'You've upset me now' says Christian. 'No more clients this afternoon!'

Obeying The One he looks through his cloak, but all it contains is the dirty old lump. Outside, the sun is setting. Oboes and trumpets start to blare. An emir, unfortunately, has the right to a military band outside his house.

Christian is holding the lump to his nose, trying to guess its origin, when a strange thing happens: an invisible force grabs his elbow and forces his fist down his throat. He gags, and swallows the lump.

Sunset; ugh. Christian goes to the rosegarden. They lock the gates, but you can climb the fence. The universe contracts, or something. He sits near the fountain. The night is soft as velvet. The scent of roses fills the air. The sky is studded with strange stars. Somewhere a woman sings.

Christian's mouth is dry, he swallows. His throat is dry, he swallows again. His heart thumps, he's dying. He needs a drink.

The fountain tastes like no water ever tasted before. Our Water, thinks Christian. He looks up at the gaping wound in the breast of the marble bird. Our Bird, he thinks. The scent of roses races to his olfactory bulbs. Our Roses, thinks Christian. Our Sacred Heart. Our Song. Our Sky. Our Stars. Our City.

He has arrived in Damcar. For the rest of the night he sits there, staring and thinking.

He wakes the next morning back in Damascus. The sound of the first bird tells him. He opens one eye and the mundane sights make him want to throw up.

14

He doesn't return to the parlour immediately, but spends the day wandering the city. His head feels fuzzy. A dozen times he passes the Piebald Palace, and each time he sees it his head empties. What a sight!

When at last he does return, he's in for a nasty shock. The Sugar Turk, annoyed at having been kept waiting, has him seized and sold to a slaver *en route* from the Land of the Black Sheep. And while it's not so bad to be a white slave in Damascus in 1394 (every soldier, every emir, even the Sultan is formally a slave), Christian is far too old to train as a soldier, and has to be sold as a 'special.'

He's less than delighted to learn his buyer is none but that notorious sadist and pervert Ismail, who kicked his arse for littering roses with Vegetable Stone.

As befits an emir of one hundred, Ismail al Dhahiri lives in fine style. As well as one hundred Mamelukes, fifty of whom are specials, he has seven wives, twelve concubines, forty-one white eunuchs and twenty-nine black slaves. The black slaves wear white and the white slaves wear black. The concubines wear pearl diadems. He has dancers, musicians, cooks, vintners, ostlers, and, of course, gatekeepers.

The emir's palace – only sultans have palaces, but what's in a name – includes barracks, stables, hall of justice, pavilion, racecourse, quarters for personal retainers (harem), castle and mosque. The whole complex belonged to a clerk in the former administration, who used it as a townhouse. The emir grabbed it following Barkuk's accession to the sultanate in Cairo. Ismail is a former cupbearer to Barkuk, and like him, a Circassian. That is, more of a special than a soldier.

The day after Christian's arrival the Mamelukes convene by the hall. There's a strong distinction between the appearance of the special Mamelukes and the military. The latter wear coloured coats, boots with spurs, fur hats, and range in age from sixteen to sixty. They are bandy, coarse, pock-marked, battle-scarred, illiterate, and bound by allegiance. They bear bows, swords, maces and lances, and with few exceptions, are Kipchak Turks.

The former, by contrast, are bare-headed boys of Circassian or Frankish origin, gorgeously dressed in blood-red or snow-white garments inscribed with the signs of the planets. Christian alone wears black, and stands to one side.

At Ismail's emergence from the hall of justice wearing his robes of honour – outer robes of scarlet satin, inner robes of yellow satin, cloak of miniver, gold brocade skullcap, gold belt, gold sword, gold scabbard – the specials cry. Their faces are daubed with kohl and belladonna. In their hands they carry cups, goblets, candlestick holders and fly whisks.

'Enough of that whimpering' says the emir. 'I find I have too many specials. I must place you in the scales and see who's wanting!'

He claps, and a pair of blindfold Nubians stumble from the hall bearing scales. From another direction appear three white maidens bearing pillows. On one pillow is a copy of the *Koran*, on another the *Torah*, on the third the *Pistis Sophia*.

The Mamelukes are weighed and the emir notes their weights. Christian is last. He can't help observing the Kipchaks are treating the whole thing as a big joke.

The emir performs some complex computations, then calls for his personal catamite. His personal catamite is a blond-haired, blue-eyed boy, frozen with terror.

'You're it' says Ismail. 'Do you know your lines?'

You know your lines, you're not nailed to the plank.

'Right' says Ismail, clapping his hands. 'Let Our Pageant commence!'

To Christian he gives a well-thumbed set of notes, entitled 'Hemicorporectomy.' 'Bone up on these' he says. 'You'll be needing them.'

The unfortunate Mameluke whose place Christian takes goes off into the palace, escorted by some military. The rest of the military return to barracks. Christian, five other Mamelukes and a concubine are taken to the hall of justice by eunuchs, and dressed as follows: one to represent Saturn, one to represent Jupiter, one to represent Mars, one to represent Venus, one to represent Luna, one to represent Mercury.

A trumpet sounds. Led by the eunuchs, the principals walk to the pavilion. The pavilion consists of gardens in which roam pheasant and peacock, pools in which swim waterfowl, and jasmine-scented trees, from which depend, in gilded cages, bulbuls and finches.

A fence is built around part of the stream. The emir, dressed in a Roman toga and ill-fitting skullcap, stands beside it. His personal catamite, dressed in all colours of the rainbow, stands nearby.

Christian, dressed as Saturn, has to go up and say 'Why is the spring closed?'

'The Spring is exclusively for the King' replies Ismail.

'And what is the colour of the king?' asks Christian, which seems a pretty stupid question.

'The King wears a golden garment, a black cuirass, a white garment, and His blood is red.'

The doomed Mameluke approaches, wearing a gold crown.

'How old is the king?' asks Christian.

'Older than the Spring itself.'

The king removes his golden cloak and gives it to Saturn, as played by Christian. He then removes his black cuirass and gives it to Jupiter, who hands it to Luna. He then removes his white garment and gives it to Mars, which leaves him naked.

He then loses his composure and runs screaming from the pavilion. Eunuchs give chase.

Ismail tears off his skullcap and dashes it to the ground. 'Another pageant ruined' he explains. 'The King has no fear of dying! Won't *anyone* die a significant death? It puts you ahead when you get where you're going.'

'Anyway' he continues, 'the bath enables the King to give His slaves His power.'

The naked king is dragged back in, and stretched across the fence. The servant of the king then takes the golden sword from beneath his toga, and starts hacking the king's waist, so the king's blood runs into the spring. When the king is dead, or almost, his servant the emir runs panting into the bushes and re-emerges dressed as the King, complete with cuirass and crown.

'Rex redivivus' he gasps. Then he grabs a goblet and fills it with blood.

At this, Christian loses composure and falls to the ground in a faint.

'*He*'s not hip' says Ismail with scorn. 'All that money I paid!'

Personal retainers sleep in a large hall with an opening in the roof and a door through which eunuchs come and go. All retainers wear black and white striped pyjamas, and sleep in chains. The chaining and unchaining of Mamelukes by eunuchs provides an opportunity for intercourse.

An hour after lights out the emir Ismail enters the hall on a black and white warhouse. He prances round, and after a swig at the bottle hanging round the horse's neck, rides over to Christian, who's sleeping, and dreaming, strange to say, of his father's castle. But that's not dreaming.

'Sleeper awake' shouts the emir, causing the horse to rear up. 'Seminate aurum vestrum in terram albam foliatam!'

The horse comes down heavily on its front legs, chipping the marble. When Christian wakes, he thinks at first it's a unicorn.

'Don't worry' says Ismail, as the two ride off. 'I'm not so fussy when drunk. There's an occult matter, buried in the depths of a fountain, vile, abject, and valued not at all, covered in excrement, to which all names are given, but only one belongs.'

'Don't tell me *you're* a Seeker after Truth as well' says Christian.

'Of course I am' says Ismail. 'I had a most unhappy childhood.'

Somehow or other, Christian has lost everything now, save his self-respect. He has no way of getting to Rhodes, no way of getting to Damcar. He's a slave in a large palace, subject to unnatural acts. Still, as the emir puts it, 'It is good for a man that he bear the yoke in his youth; that way he can blame all subsequent bad behaviour on his childhood.'

Christian decides to confide in the emir, with whom, for the present, he spends most nights.

'I see. And you know who invented the Vegetable Stone? The Assassins.'

'What happened to them?'

They and their proteges the Templars, were driven out by Sultan Baybars. He also outlawed the Vegetable Stone, or "assass", as it's known to the vulgar.'

'Baybars? The man who built the Piebald Palace?'

'That's him, a hard-liner. Actually, you could probably get some assass through the Brotherhood, but I'm tired of this conversation; let's get to business. You're going to come, if it kills me!'

Christian is ordered to cry, bleed and sweat every day for a week. The first is achieved by forcing him to watch one of the military Mamelukes being halved at the waist for writing on the wall of the viceroy's palace 'The Wazeer is a low Coptic clerk.' This, in association with pay claims. The man is quite illiterate. The emir gives as his reason for punishment, 'The Prophet forbids persecution of Christians.'

Friday evening after prayers a cord is let through the opening in the roof. After seven minutes a bell rings and the cord is drawn up again. No one takes much notice, even Christian, till one Friday the emir causes a couch to be brought into hall, on which he reclines, eating an apple, and staring at the hole.

The cord is duly lowered.

'Anyone who can climb that cord and reach the roof is free' says a man. 'But don't try it, Christian; I witnessed the last two bids. They shake the cord and it's a long way down, to a marble floor.'

I've fallen off walls in my time, thinks Christian. Shall I give it a go?

Too late. The bell rings and the cord is hauled up. The emir tosses his apple core over his shoulder, and says to Christian, 'Next week last chance.' He belches and leaves.

By next Friday, Christian's mind is made up. The place is more brutal than a Franciscan cloister.

Fit pullo a nido volans, qui iterum cadit in nidum.

As soon as the cord is let down, Christian heads straight for it. The whole assembly, eunuchs, emir and mamelukes, make small wagers. Rhinoceros to win, Unicorn the danger. Christian, heavily chained but unpinned, arrives at the cord as the bell rings. He takes the cord between both hands, and finds it made of silk, alas. There's no sign of a man above, only the constellations. The rope starts moving, accompanied by a loud banging noise. Christian seizes the rope and winds it round his hands. The loud banging noise increases; he's never noticed that before.

When he's ten feet off the ground and wondering whether to continue, he realizes the loud banging noise comes not from the roof, but the door. Person or persons unknown are seeking admittance to the hall. The eunuchs are frightened. No one looks at Christian now. Shouting is heard.

When Christian is twenty feet off the floor, the point of no return in one piece, the door breaks and the military Mamelukes, all forty-nine of them, rush in. A cry goes up from every eunuch, every special, the emir himself. The military Mamelukes are wielding scimitars and shouting at the top of their voices. The emir jumps on top of the couch and tries to regain authority. He tries to draw his sword, but it's stuck in that scabbard again.

He should have found the right scabbard while he had the chance, thinks Christian.

A group of Mamelukes fall on the hated emir with swords drawn. Christian looks away: the cord is getting slippery. Thirty feet off the floor now, almost half-way up.

He tries to concentrate on the ceiling, but finds he grips better looking down. The military Mamelukes are busily halving decadent specials at the waist. The marble floor is awash in blood.

Ten feet to go. Whoever's hauling feels no fear or holds great pride in his work. The rope starts swinging violently, feet from the top: the final test.

Christian looks down. The military Mamelukes are hacking at corpses, reluctant to leave. Some engage in acts of vandalism, chipping the walls with their filthy spurs.

Christian is through the hole now, gashed where his head struck the pigeon loft. The man helping him from his chains wears a golden fleece and a green inner robe. He's not a Turk, but has well-developed biceps.

'What do you think of that?' he says, lying down, looking through the hole.

'I can't think' says Christian, 'I've a splitting headache.'

'As a man soweth, that shall he reap. Because his patron murdered *his* patron, his Mamelukes have murdered him.'

'These nobles are all the same' says Christian, thinking of his father, spitefully. The man grabs him and holds him over the hole.

'No they're not' he says. 'I want you to make a promise to your dead benefactor before you leave this roof.'

'As you like' says Christian, in no position to argue.

'In gratitude to your dead benefactor, you must add his name to yours. And in gratitude to the Prophet, you must take *His* name as yours. And in contrition for the evil life you've led, you must drop your name entirely. Your name is now Mohammad Ismaili.'

Fancy being grateful to Ismail, thinks Christian: How absurd!

With the election of a new emir, Yalbugha al Ismaili, it's safe to climb down. Confirmation of loyalty is sent to Cairo by pigeon post. The gatekeeper is also pigeon keeper. He never shuts his eyes. Christian walks out the main gate, taking leave of his friend as he goes.

'We'll meet again' says the gatekeeper, 'by my outer golden fleece and inner robe of green.'

'I doubt that' says Christian, smiling. 'But thanks for your kindness in any event.'

Now for the Brotherhood! (Friend, do you love the Goldmaker's Art? Surprise and ecstasy are in store for you!)

15

All that people want to discuss, however, is Tamerlane crossing the Tigris.

'God help us' they say, 'when he took Baghdad there wasn't a stone left standing!'

'Now about this Brotherhood' Christian persists.

One day while Christian is crawling along with others near the rosegarden, throwing dust in his hair for contrition, the Sugar Turk happens by.

'Get up' he says. 'We employ Syrians for that sort of thing. You're supposed to be a Mameluke!'

'What do you know of the Brotherhood?' asks Christian. He never lets up.

The Sugar Turk drags him from the gutter by his ears, and beats him soundly. 'Don't let me hear that talk' he says. 'There's no Brotherhood, there's just *me*! Me me me, and me mater.'

Many of the mob cheer at this, and some get off their knees.

'Wonderful' says an elderly abbot. 'There's guts in the army yet.' The Sugar Turk walks off smiling and Christian gets up coughing blood.

'That was an unchristian act' asserts Christian, 'and you approve?'

'Of course I approve' says the abbot. 'We employ Turks to

behave in an unchristian way. The outer circle must protect the inner.'

I've got the wrong city here, thinks Christian. Damcar, that's the place!

Sultan Barkuk arrives from Cairo with the full army a week later. Christian, from the rosegarden, watches them ride past. Thirty thousand mounted men, dressed in silk, satin, silver and gold. I wonder what *that*'d look like in Damcar, thinks Christian. Terrific, I imagine. Many Damascans join the train of baggage camels to watch the fight. It'll be some fight, the long-awaited clash of the world's two greatest armies.

Christian elects to stay behind and finds work carting dung to an orchard.

'Make every post a winning post' says the Jewish owner of the orchard. 'Armies can be good for business. I bought out my neighbours cheap, and the streets are full of horseshit. So far I'm laughing.'

Christian's laughing too. He has money in his purse again, fruit in his belly, and not a Frank or Turk to obstruct him.

'Ever heard of the Brotherhood?' he asks. 'Or where I might buy pure mercury?'

'You disappoint me' says the Jew. 'I was going to make you a partner. I said to myself, here's a nice style of boy with a future in the business world.'

When Christian returns to the city, he finds it in a state of jubilation. Everywhere people are laughing and dancing, and wooden towers are being erected on street corners, draped with carpets. Houses are decked in silk and jewels. 'What's going on?' he inquires.

'Haven't you heard?' says a whirling dervish, whirling. 'The Mongols backed off!'

The brothels and wine bars are waiting ready when the army returns next day. The young Mamelukes, who aren't keen to fight the Mongols, are relieved. Their relief takes the form of youthful exuberance, looting, rape, and so on. The old Mamelukes, aching for battle, are bitterly disappointed; they sit morosely drinking, spitting on the footpath and picking fights.

Tamerlane has the sense to see, that if he bides his time, these old Mamelukes will soon be dead and their place taken by the young ones.

Sometimes the old Mamelukes get a bite from their insults, and killing ensues. Christian gets work removing bodies from in front of a wine shop and taking bets. Most of the Mamelukes buy him drinks as well, and he's soon forgotten mercury.

'Mohammad' one maudlin old Kipchak says every time Christian passes, 'have a drink on me. I wanted to die a martyr in battle, and this was my last chance. How would I be?'

'A Moslem shouldn't be drinking fermented mare's milk' says Christian disapprovingly.

'*Moslem*! Don't make me choke. They've seventy-eight monasteries in this city, Mohammad, and notice something? The more these characters pray, the worse our situation gets.'

Nonetheless, Fridays, everyone goes to the opulent mosque, even Christian. The original Medina mosque was a mud hut with a palm roof, but this one was built centuries later by a Mameluke sultan with a guilty conscience.

'Allah's tired of your bad behaviour' says the shaikh, 'there's been an outbreak of disease.'

The mosque empties in minutes. Old Mamelukes and indigenes are immune to the plague, but not so young Mamelukes: they will die like flies.

The army returns to Cairo, leaving a city showing signs of wear, but nothing to what could have been; Mongols not only depopulate cities, but dismantle them, stone by stone.

The wine shops close, and Christian returns to hospital to dry out. The doctors put him in a ward of Egyptian disease, not knowing he's had it.

Everyone in the ward dies horribly, except Christian alone. On the morning of the third day he's reading the paper when he comes upon the following advertisement:

'Chemist wanted: inexperienced man preferred.'

16

'What job are you here for?' says the master. 'Fraud-squad trainee or chemist?'

It's not a bad sort of house; central, not far from the rosegarden. Christian must have passed it a thousand times looking for the Brotherhood.

'Sit down' says the master. He goes away and returns with a pot of Chinese tea smelling strongly of sulphur. Sulphur is an oleaginous body composed of subtle earth saturated with water and a fat unctuous airy humidity capable of being fused by heat and coagulated by cold. It has three humours, two superfluous and one necessary. Purge the superfluous, purify the necessary, and you have what you need.

'I like the way you're sitting' says the master, 'it augurs well. Half my students become chemists, the rest members of the fraud squad. Tell me which stream interests you, and I'll adapt my tea room conversation to suit. The lab work's identical.'

After a meal of curds, the master leads Christian to a room with a small bed in one corner, lit by a candle on the wall. In the middle of the room is a tub on which lies a tripod, a bucket and a large brush. Hundreds of items of dirty apparatus lie on the stone floor, stacked in places to the roof.

'Fires may be lit from dung' says the master, 'and smoke expelled with a flapping towel. More than that I can't say, but here are some books you may find of interest. I'll leave you to it.'

* * *

Night sessions for the fraud squad, day sessions for the chemists. No fraternization. Chemist's nights are free, or as the master puts it, 'I can't force you, but if you want to impress by hard work and enthusiasm, do.' There are several other students, all Syrian. They suppose Christian a locally-born Turk, and ignore him; he doesn't disabuse them.

Before sunrise, Christian is in the streets to find dung for his fires. From breakfast till tea he works scrubbing his apparatus, with frequent rests on the bed, it being understood no student can proceed till his apparatus is clean. Suits me, thinks Christian, I don't *want* to proceed: I just need somewhere to sleep.

All breakages are replaced. Scouring with salt and sand, rinsing with acid, scalding with water, Christian makes slow progress, but eventually has only the one large, black, cauldron left. This defies all his efforts to break it, being made of iron, and he dare not purge its quicksilver harshly, for fear of converting it to copper.

The Syrian students, by this stage, are all embarked on more interesting work; Christian finds tea-room conversation increasingly difficult to follow.

'Chemistry' says the master, 'teaches us to cure the diseases of metals. Gold is the first and true intention of Nature with regard to metals. Iron has leprosy of the bile, copper has leprosy of the blood. Tin has phlegmatic leprosy, while lead is more of your melancholic leper. Tell us, Abdul, what have we learnt in our experiments on the nature of sulphur and quicksilver?'

'Sulphur' says Abdul, 'is various; it may be white, yellow, saffron or black. Quicksilver is always the same.'

'And the inference?'

'The sickly pallor of leprous metals is due to sulphur.'

'Correct. Our Medicine, like Nature, separates off the corrupting sulphur. Tell them why, Neshu.'

'Sulphur doesn't mix with gold' says Neshu. 'Mercury does.

The inference is that gold contains no sulphur.'

'Correct. Metals are composed of water, that is, mercury, and hot dry earth, that is, sulphur. In human generation a powerful sperm with enough heat to quench all menstrual blood, produces a male. A weak sperm a female. That's why a female has less natural heat than a male, and a daughter is so disgraceful. Every felt the inside of a woman's snatch boys? Talk about cold and wet – but I've got ahead of myself here; we'll leave that for the blindfold test between the slavegirl and the salamander.'

One thing for sure, thinks Christian, brooding over his futile search. If ever *I* form a society, there'll be nothing secret about it.

Christian finally cleans his cauldron (with urine) and is given a project. The master asks him to bring his cauldron into the yard, and there, by a plum tree, with the snowy peak of Mt Hermon in the distance, explains.

'Science is possible because the Cosmos is the work of an Intelligence to which reason corresponds. The generation and corruption of everything, including metals, is, in the traditional view, under control of the heavenly bodies. These in turn are under the direct control of this Intelligence.'

'You mean Allah' says Christian.

'Call it what you will. Now in the traditional view, the influences which determine whether the vital spark in a metal produces gold, are unknown, if not unknowable. As you know, Nature has two ways of producing gold: the immediate method, by which mercury is changed at once to gold, and the mediate method, by which mercury is converted first to lead, then iron, then bronze, and so on. Art is supposed to imitate Nature in the second method, for of course, as Geber says, if Nature did *not* change common metals into gold, then all the efforts of Our Art would be in vain.

'Please take notes. Just as gold can be made in two ways, by mediate or immediate method, so with some plants and animals. Examples are mice, beetles and wasps, as compared to say, palm trees and vipers, which are produced by generation only, and lice and earthworms, which are produced by putrefaction only. Production of mostly generable animals by putrefaction depends on the fortuitous combination of the same elements by which that animal is normally produced. Aristotle, it is true, maintains that such animals are not the same as those generated normally, but I think we can prove otherwise. A far more interesting problem is what part, if any, the heavenly bodies play in this putrefaction. Examples of putrefaction occur in the mineral world as well; iron is sometimes made from thunderbolts in black clouds. Alemanic swords are made of this iron, when it falls to earth, and I can give you references that prove such iron is identical with iron produced in mines, except of course, it is harder, being made by the rapid desiccation of aerial fire.

'Evidence exists that putrefaction proceeds independent of celestial influence, but a thorough study, to my knowledge, has not yet been attempted. If we can show that wasps are produced by putrefaction in ass carcasses at a rate dependent on warmth, but independent of the season of the year, and moreover that such wasps breed indiscriminately with wasps made by generation, we shall have gone some way towards vindicating Rhases' statement that, in the Magisterium, *ceteris paribus*, the stellar influence is not important.'

Fresh ass meat can be bought at the market. The cauldron is placed under plum trees, surrounded by water, sand, dung or fire, and the time noted for the appearance of the first wasps.

Certain precautions have to be taken to preclude contamination of the cauldron. Christian's old black burnous is burnt and replaced with a fresh white robe, for instance.

How boring. The wasps are hard to find because of all the worms. Christian spends most of his time in his cell, reading, dreaming and thinking.

'You keep to yourself too much' says the master. 'Why don't

you join the Mosque Younger Set? I understand they're a delightful group of charming young people.'

Christian declines; he can't imagine anything more abhorrent.

'You'll have to do something more with yourself than lie about all day. I think I'll start you on a preparation of the Mineral Stone.'

'What about the *Vegetable* Stone?' says Christian.

'Keep your mind above your thorax! The first thing we must do is dissolve our Golden Sun in our Green Lion: for the true beginning of Our Work is in the solution of the body; bodies when dissolved become spiritual, and as the sages say, unless the body becomes incorporeal, and the spirit corporeal, no progress can be made. A dissolved body is still more fixed than its spirit, though dissolved with it. For the solution of the body means the coagulation of the spirit, and vice versa. Understand this, and you have the arcanum.'

'What about the *Vegetable* Stone?'

'For dissolution, unparalleled: but that's only half the story.'

Can this be the Mosque Younger Set? Half a dozen ruffians slouched on a carpet in an outhouse.

'Who are you and what do you want?'

'My name is Mohammad Ismaili. I want to fill in my evenings.'

'Basically, we're anti-corruption and anti-Circassian. Do you love Allah and hate hypocrisy?'

'I hate hypocrisy.'

'We'll admit you as half member. That gives you the right to listen but not speak.'

'Ah, don't admit him at all' says an ugly Kipchak. 'I'll bet he's corrupt.'

They admit him though, on a show of hands. Need the numbers and can't count. Most of the set are unemployed sons of Mameluke fathers, who can't join the army. A Mameluke has to have had an unhappy childhood, and the son of a Mameluke hasn't. Every night they meet to discuss corruption; when they can think of someone sufficiently corrupt, they go out and beat him.

'Always plenty of wine for the army.'

'What about Barkuk? *There*'s an hypocrite.'

'*Sultan*! You realize he was a special? A cupbearer who murdered his patron?'

'Can't fight and never could. Circassians are corrupt. They bring all their relatives out and put them straight in the army, no training. Half of them can't ride a horse.'

Moan, gripe. On the last day of the Magisterium, the operator becomes one with his material. Look at me, he says, I'm laughing!

We say he's crying, but it'll do him good.

Christian is making notes one night when the ugly Kipchak snatches his paper.

'Ah' he says, 'this is fraud squad stuff. I took that course meself. All I remember is Avicenna proved it.'

'Proved what?'

'That lead can't be turned to gold!'

Aha! The penny drops. The master is saying one thing to chemists, another to the fraud squad! Talk about two-faced!

Christian decides to confront him at once. The master's study is lined with books, many Arabic, some Greek, some Latin. The master listens and smiles.

'Yes, it's true' he admits. 'Avicenna *did* deny the possibility of transmutation.'

'That's not what you told *us*' says Christian. 'You said he was the greatest chemist that ever lived!'

'So he was. Listen Christian – Mohammad I mean – this is premature. The flour fight between the fraud squad and the chemistry school is scheduled for the breaking-up party. Not many last that long. At this stage, all I will say is that metals are made of sulphur and mercury, and that sulphur contains mercury, and that mercury contains sulphur. Had Avicenna said *other* than the opposite of what he said, then we'd have cause for concern. As it is, he said one thing, but also the opposite: Method of the Sages. You have no idea of how extraordinarily difficult this can be. In the beginning we expect, as well as what we expect, the opposite. Later on we expect both, that is, we expect nothing. There are two worlds, Mohammad, the sun and its shadow, the sulphur and its mercury, and they can take up two orientations, like bipoles in a magnetic field. Consequently there's always a bit of sun in the shadow, and always a bit of shadow in the sun. To fight is to fight, but a fighter may flee.'

'All right' says Christian, 'if to fight is to flee, then why does sulphur fight and mercury flee?'

'Good question. Because they have been taught to do so. But one who knew the arcanum could teach them otherwise. Imagine, Christian – if you could make mercury fight and sulphur flee!'

Christian is not the only half member of the Younger Set; there's another, a quiet, lacklustre fellow, who sits in the corner and won't come on raids. One night, shortly after resurrecting sugar, with his leprosy, all over the fluted filter papers, Christian is accosted by this youth, while scouring the back of the Mosque for broken tiles to take on a raid against old women who sell cabbage at high prices.

'Feel like joining the Brotherhood?'

'Our wolf is found in the East and our dog in the West; the one bites the other, and the other bites back, and they both become furious and mutually kill each other, till the poison originates from them as well as the medicine.'

Rhases, Light of Lights

'Ah there you are' says the master. 'I didn't see you at the meeting, and wondered where you'd got to. A man called by earlier looking for Christian Rosy Cross.'

'Oh. Did you tell him there was no one here by that name?'

'I did, but he wouldn't believe me. He left this calling card.'

The master produces the card; it's the rind off a tree, blue-stained. In golden print it bears a single world, *Congratulator*.

'Gee' says Christian, 'I wonder what for?'

'Never mind' says the master, 'don't take it to heart. Now then, back to work. You say you have the sugar through the holes but he won't rise up? When resurrecting purified bodies, Christian, we have need of two things; heat and timing.'

'Please don't call me Christian' says Christian. 'The name's Mohammad.'

The master laves the calling card, and Christian turns it over. It bears on the back a single word in black, *Condoleo*.

17

The rosegarden, 3 a.m., stipulates the card.

By the fountain sits a gatekeeper, cross-legged, with a happy smile, and in front of him a piece of chemical apparatus Christian recognizes; a wide-arm distillation flask, half-filled with petals and water.

Next day, the master is not impressed. 'You say the aim of this lodge is to keep gates and tell truth?'

'Yes, but it's more important than it sounds. Learn to keep a gate correctly, and you have the arcanum.'

'No doubt. Mind telling me what's so great about gatekeeping?'

'The Vegetable Stone. They have it.'

'They would. And you prefer dirty old assass to Mineral Stone?'

'After two hookahs' explains Christian, 'I threw away my staff and walked normally.'

'Round in small circles, no doubt. Well, are you going to stay here?'

'For the time being. Can I go on the gate?'

'We have no gate Mohammad. But you're welcome to stand by the door in the yard, provided you do your homework first.'

* * *

You have to be a Moslem to join the Gatekeeper's Lodge, there's no getting round it. When the hierophant – Christian's old friend, Yalburgha's gatekeeper – accepts Christian, he makes a proviso of admission to the Faith.

'Go the Mosque' he says. 'Ask for the Shaikh. It's just a convention, *we* don't care, but our funding comes from pillage. They're fussy how we give it away, you understand. Now you're certain you were never a Christian?'

'Positive' says Christian. 'I went through a form of baptism, but the man who did it was an heretic.'

'Right, there should be no problem. You don't need special credentials. A strong back, and you've got it. Penis two feet long a bonus. Good lungs. The most important thing you'll learn is who to let through the gate. Once you've learnt that, you're eligible for the Brotherhood.'

'And then I get to smoke more Stone?'

'Oh no; that's when you give it away. What line of work are you in, Mohammad?'

'Chemist's assistant.'

'I see. Solve and coagulate. Well I think we can promise to turn you into a very dissolute person.'

'Just as I feared' says the master.

Mohammad's a Moslem. With the prospect of a trip to Damcar, he's memorized the *Koran* in an afternoon.

'What's the matter *now*?' explodes Christian. 'You're always saying dissolution is the first part of Our Art!'

'I know, but if you're not dissolute, who is? And do you really want what you really want?'

'That depends' says Christian. 'I know I'm tired of my deformity!'

'You fool, you don't know *half* of it! You never did get that castle of yours! And once you start on the Vegetable Stone, forget it. Forget everything! It's the most dangerous way of making Laton white there is. You know, in the old days, when Baybars purged the assassins, he picked up Hassan i Sabbah by random quartering at the thorax. The sooty lung led to the mountain stronghold. The very way they took you off me stinks! I'll put in a complaint at the next general meeting.'

'What do you mean?'

'What would happen if I went round handing out Mineral Stone?'

'You're just jealous' says Christian.

'Jealous of *that* riff raff? Don't make me cough.'

'Their biceps are bigger than yours, and people trust appearances.'

18

Now in this Work you finish up where you start out. That's why it's important you start out in the right place.

During his initiation, Christian observes that lodge members fall into two groups; heavily-muscled gatekeepers, but also some rather patrician-looking men, who keep to themselves, as far to one side of the fountain as gatekeepers to the other.

When Christian asks the novice next to him, a Mameluke called Sal, who these are, Sal replies that these are emirs of one hundred.

'Emirs of one hundred!'

'Sure' says Sal. 'What would you expect, in the lodge of the emirs?'

It's 3 a.m. and cold, mid-winter. The seven novices, each selected during the previous year, stand in groups. Christian is in his own category, the category of 'Raven'. The other categories are 'Raven and Dove', 'Dove' and 'Neither Raven nor Dove', but of these 'Dove' and 'Neither Raven nor Dove' are empty.

When sponsors are called for, there's hissing and booing from the emirs, as the Grand Gatekeeper, the gatekeeper to the emir Yalbugha, walks over to Christian.

'Emirs of one hundred' he explains to Christian, face red with embarrassment. 'The latest lodge, you understand. We two had the least in common, and had to make the merger. Orders of the annual general meeting. You've been married, haven't you?'

'No' says Christian, 'never been married.'

'That's what I told them, but they won't believe a word I say.'

'Shut up' says the hierophant of the emirs, who's taking over. 'Bring out the Cross!'

The cross is produced. 'I thought we were supposed to be Moslems' says Christian.

'We are' says the Gatekeeper. 'Decadent types! Fortunately, my emir Yalbugha has no interest in The Truth. He's the kind of Turk we expect a Turk to be.'

'Novices who undergo successful Ordeal of the Cross' says the Grand Emir, 'will each receive a Rose.'

'Who *is* he?' asks Christian. There can be no doubt, the Grand Emir is a fine-looking man.

'Viceroy of Damascus' says the Grand Gatekeeper. 'Tanam al Dhahiri the Reticent. I ask you.'

Each novice is taken forward by his sponsor, to kiss the Cross and swear oaths. As Christian is presented, the viceroy smiles at him from the fountain steps.

'I must admit I'm most impressed by your choice of the name "Christian Rosy Cross." Tell me, whatever made you select it?'

Given the option of starting with either tutor, Christian chooses the viceroy. On the way to the palace, he remembers something about a vow of secrecy. Too late; he's already told everyone.

He comforts himself that *real* secrecy is believing something no one else does.

The audience chamber stands at the end of an open court with trees in tubs. The viceroy's throne is up one end, hidden from the eye by curtains. Waiting in the courtyard, Christian wonders how he's ever going to get in. Hundreds of citizens queue three deep, waiting to air their grievances. Some are so aggrieved, they can't sleep at night.

Christian tries to push his way in, but vigorously repelled, joins the queue. The gatekeeper, recognizing him, winks, but Christian does not wink back; he's starting to regret his decision not to start with his Grand Gatekeeper.

Finally, a tall man wearing bath robe and slippers shuffles up – the viceroy. No one recognizes him, he looks so different out of regalia. It takes an hour and a half just to get it on and off.

With a wave to the gatekeeper, the viceroy motions for Christian to follow him. A smelly old door next to the dump leads to a secret passage, and a door at the far end of this passage leads to a secret library.

Tracking lettuce leaves and old pieces of fruit onto the floor, the viceroy speaks of the man who built the palace with great respect.

'But I couldn't let on who it was' he says. 'Vows of secrecy – you understand. And now, if you'll excuse me, I must see what's happening in Mugsville.'

He opens a secret panel in the wall, which opens on the back of the throne room. There's a colossal noise from the audience chamber, with someone accusing someone of extortion. The viceroy actuates a lever, causing a pair of mechanical hands to clap. Next complainant, please.

'I was having trouble with the mechanism, and got the gatekeeper to fix it. It turned out he's read most of the books in my library! I was aghast.'

'What about a smoke before we start' says Christian.

'Oh very well' says the viceroy. In a compartment of the throne room wall is a huge and venerable hookah.

'I can perfectly understand your resentment towards gatekeepers' says the viceroy. From time to time he actuates the clapping lever, keeping things moving.

'Aren't you frightened someone will open the curtains?' asks Christian. 'And I never said I resent gatekeepers; on the contrary, I respect them.'

'They wouldn't do that' says the viceroy. 'More than their lives are worth. Besides, they don't want to listen, they only want to talk.'

'No, I can understand how you feel about gatekeepers all right. We interest them as far as possible in religion, to stop them reproducing. Cheaper than cutting their balls out, with none of the harmful side effects. Which brings me to another point I worked out this morning: do you realize I take home less pay than my own gatekeeper? And look at the mouths I have to feed. I'm not interested in money, Mohammad, I know money's worthless. I don't want any more money than the next fellow, unless that fellow's my gatekeeper. What does *he* do for his money, I'd like to know? Opens the gate in the morning and shuts it again at night!'

'It's heavy' says Christian.

'I'm not denying that' says the viceroy. 'I'm not saying, cut him off without a denar. What I'm saying is, why should I get less money than he does? Oh I know 100,000 a month sounds a lot, but the men are screaming, they say they can't turn out for less than 1,000. Besides, we soldiers risk our necks.'

'Speaking of necks' says Christian, 'any chance of a glass of water?'

'We risk our necks! We ride into battle on horses that cost twice what they should! I'm in the front! I tell you straight, I won't take on the Mongols for less than a gatekeeper's wage. You're a Mameluke, you understand. Why should *we* risk our necks, while our Syrian slaves are laughing, safe and sound behind the gate.'

'According to them' says Christian, '*we*'re the slaves.'

'Is *that* what they're saying? By God, that does it!'

White with anger, the viceroy opens the door and assumes the throne. As luck would have it, a wealthy horse trader and outfitter is complaining of the cost of raw leather.

'Enough' shouts the reticent viceroy. 'Seize this man and confiscate his goods!'

It's no sooner said than done. The viceroy then gives his gatekeeper some work, by dismissing the crowd 'till further notice.'

'I don't know what you see in this stuff' says the viceroy, exhaling. 'It makes me walk into doors.'

'It relaxes me' says Christian, enjoying the sensation of a flaccid penis. On the ceiling, strange patterns form. The yard, with its cauldron in it. The pines of home. That trek with Pal – what an *exciting* life it had been!

'It might have been best to cut out their balls' admits the

viceroy, 'but then they get lazy. The trouble is, sexual energy can be tapped in other ways.'

'Did you hear what I said, Mohammad? I said sexual energy can be tapped in other ways!'

'I hear you' says Christian, 'I know. I've seen a portrait of Thomas Aquinas.'

Outside in the yard again, Christian wonders where he is. Having worked it out, he takes a step, and wonders where he is again.

So it continues. No sooner has he worked out where he is, than he's working out where he is again.

By the time he reaches the gate, it's nigh on dusk. The gatekeeper takes one look at him and laughs. 'By gee he's an old scoundrel, Mohammad, but his number's up. Take a look at this!'

The gatekeeper has the gate barred with his strong arms. Without, is a howling mob. Christian watches it a while, then goes away to climb the back fence. Passing the dump, he sees the viceroy emerge from the back passage, this time in full regalia. Christian waves, but the viceroy ignores him.

He's probably forgotten who I am, thinks Christian. Come to think of it, who am I?

As he climbs the wall, he notices something odd in the behaviour of the iron spikes. They're talking. He notices the same thing again with the iron in his cell that night. He can't sleep, but listens all night to what the iron has to say.

We're all right, mate. There's nothing wrong with us.

'Now look here Christian' says the master later that day, 'I'm afraid it won't wash. I'll put in a further complaint at the annual general meeting!'

'What's wrong *now*?' says Christian, making a first appearance at afternoon tea.

'Sleeping by day is unnatural!'

'I've been awake all night!'

I don't know what to do, thinks Christian. His chemistry's bullshit, but how can I tell him?

I don't know what to do, thinks the master. He's ripe for the fraud squad, and the chief error in this Art is haste.

'Ar, there you are' says the Grand Gatekeeper. 'So you had a torrid time with the opposite number? I'll say this for the viceroy, he takes his work seriously.'

'My word he does' says Christian.

'Unfortunately, he's obsessive. They're strange people, these slaves. We found years back the easiest way to keep them under control is to let them pretend they're in charge.'

The Gatekeeper opens the gate to admit a Mameluke from the polo match. 'A mate of mine will shortly be here to give you an exam. He used to be a big man at the Mosque, but they wound up throwing him out. He always began by getting up and saying, "Now then, are there any questions?" '

'And were there?' asks Christian. He's doing some push-ups to strengthen his arms. Practise must keep pace with theory, in this Work.

'Not as a general rule' says the Gatekeeper. 'People here think they're got the game by the throat.'

'Speaking of throats' says Christian . . .

'Wait till after your exam. What you must realize the Vegetable Stone is valuable, priceless, costly and rare.'

'Is that a fact' says Christian. 'And I was told to seek it in the dung.'

'How's that for inflation? But here comes my mate. Don't worry if you can't make head nor tail of what he says. He's years ahead of his time.'

A man approaches. It's The One, properly speaking The Two. He has such charisma that in his presence the world drifts off like a dream.

'I know him' says Christian.

'That's what we all say' says the Gatekeeper. 'He's years ahead of his time.'

Without speaking The One, properly speaking The Two,

goes into the gatehouse. He shuts the door, but Christian follows.

'The Brotherhood' says The One, who's clearly a member, 'is open to all. We explain that little paradox, ladies and gentlemen, by pointing out the All is the One. The idea is not to abandon Damascus for Damcar, but to keep a foot in both.'

'I couldn't understand a word' says Christian, after The One has left.

'No worries' says the Gatekeeper, lighting the hookah. 'That was the hipness test. I thought it worth a try, in view of your anatomical irregularity.'

'. . . anyhow, Mohammad, that's your namesake the Prophet. He wanted to join the Brotherhood, but they wouldn't let him in. You have to be a bachelor. So he sneaks in one night and what should he see on the wall but the symbol for mercury. Well, you can imagine his reaction: to him it's the devil with horns on.'

'Sorry' says Christian, 'I've lost the gist. All I can hear is the gate talking.'

There's nothing the matter with us, the gate is saying, we're perfectly all right.

When he gets home, Christian goes straight to the master's study. The master is making some notes for the fraud squad: chemists are supposed to be asleep.

'What can I do for you Christian?' says the master. He sighs, and puts away his notes.

'You can't make a horse of a dog! You can't make a man of an ape!'

'Christian; we've discussed this many times. As Geber says, metals differ, not specifically, but accidentally. All ignoble metals are potentially what gold is actually.'

'Then gold's an old man.'

'Gold is a noble man, eternal.'

'Then who's the old man? If Nature changes base metals to gold, and if base metals are children, perfect as far as they go, but not going far enough, who's the old man? If you can go far enough, you can also go too far!'

'Is that what that gatekeeper said? By God, he's gone too far this time!'

'No, I worked it out myself. If lead's a baby, gold's an old man. What's the good of gold anyway? Everyone complains about it. *Iron* is the king of the metals. *Iron* is the young man, useful in gates and fences.'

'Iron is seventeen years old, Christian. But where'd you get this theory?'

'It was given me by iron itself in Damcar, if you must know. The theory's *wrong*! Your mistake is in thinking the end product's the aim.'

When Christian has gone, the master sits in thought, then pulls out his personal files, and under the heading 'Rosencreutz, Christian' writes the date (1395) and the following entry:

'Ascended from Saturn to Mars at age seventeen, in characteristic fashion. However, strongly recommend continuation of Saturn/Jupiter: Father/Son theology, in view of the anatomical irregularity.'

Est in mari nostro pisciculus rotundus, ossibus et corticibus carens, et habet in se pinguedinem, mirificamque virtutem.

19

'The danger in this Stone, Mohammad, is that under its influence many commence transformations they can't sustain without it. And supplies are short. Now when you finish that hookah, I want you to come with me. I've got a job to do.'

The Gatekeeper takes Christian to the hall of justice. 'And don't forget what we told you' says the gate.

'We won't' says Christian.

The Gatekeeper sharpens a huge sword, in a small room.

'Is that an alemanic sword?' asks Christian.

'It is indeed. You've learnt about them in chemistry, have you?'

'Yes' says Christian. 'The iron in alemanic swords is made in the air.'

'Direct from the red planet. The Brotherhood used to make them from the Stone which Saturn vomited up, which is kept in the Kaaba. Well, I guess that'll do it. No, it's a great honour for a Mameluke to be halved at the waist with an alemanic sword. He takes it for a personal compliment.'

The door flies open. In the courtyard stand three young Mamelukes, naked to the waist. Next to them, a wheel to which another is strapped. Other Mamelukes stand around, laughing and eating apples. The Gatekeeper walks out of the hall, wielding his sword in the sun. The naked Mamelukes wail.

'All in a day's work' says the iron.

* * *

'I don't mind halving Turks at the waist' says the Gatekeeper, back at the gate. 'It doesn't hurt if you don't want it to. It can be the experience of a lifetime.'

'I think it hurt those men' says Christian, 'judging by their screams.'

'Never judge a Turk by his scream' says the Gatekeeper. 'They make the same sound when laughing. But no, you could be right, it may have hurt a bit. Especially that one I had the trouble with, the one with the strong back. But look at it this way, Mohammad, they wouldn't be suffering at all, if they hadn't been such villains in their previous existence. To start with, they wouldn't be Turks, would they? The wheel of destiny is a useful concept.'

'So it's all right to work as an executioner?'

'All right? For me, it's incumbent! I'll lend you a book called the *Bhagavad Gita*, which explains it all quite beautifully.'

'Could you do it in Damascus?'

'All the same to me, Mohammad. Damcar, Damascus, all the same. But speaking of Damcar, you've taken some Stone and put it in your pocket.'

'No' says Christian, 'but I must admit the thought occurred to me.'

Smash! The Gatekeeper flattens Christian with a blow to the jaw. 'It didn't hurt' says the gate.

'Let that be a lesson to you' says the Gatekeeper. 'In this Work, the operator becomes one with his material.'

'Ha ha' says the gate. 'You look so funny with your big bruised jaw there.'

At afternoon tea, the master inquires of Christian, has he done his day's work? 'No' says Christian, 'but I must admit I thought about it.'

The master boxes his ears. That does it, thinks Christian, I'm getting out! But he has nowhere to go.

* * *

As Hermes says, the active, working mercury, and the passive, suffering mercury, are of the same origin and the same character, as may easily be seen by the circular form of both. Hence, it is not important the inner circle is smaller than the outer, because as something becomes more hidden, it also becomes more spiritual. The smaller circle, which exists in a hidden state, then acts upon the larger circle, and makes the larger circle equal to itself.

'I thought we could start on some maths today' says the viceroy, back in the library. He's wearing a horse rug and sandals.

'I don't know any' says Christian. 'I must have been a villain in my previous existence.'

'Don't blame your previous existence, Mohammad: blame your father! Never blame yourself – always blame your father. After all, it's his fault you are the mess you are.'

Hey, that's right, thinks Christian.

'Children must be educated by their parents' continues the viceroy. 'Pliny writes of nightingales that train their young to sing. The horse teaches the foal to neigh, the dog teaches the pup to bark. Tell me, Mohammad, what did your father ever teach you?'

'Nothing' shouts Christian. 'I never thought of him before! I always blamed the prior!'

'Big mistake' says the viceroy, 'not the poor old prior's fault. *He* didn't ask to bring you up. That was your father's responsibility. I had a grouse father myself. He taught me all he knew.'

'My father spent no time with me' admits Christian.

'Oo, how disgraceful. My father taught me to light the fires, dig the tent-posts, do all the work. Then, when I was eight, and there was no more he could teach me, he sold me to a slaver, so I could enjoy the advantages here.'

'My father did *nothing* for me' shouts Christian. 'I could be in a palace bigger than this!'

'Don't worry! I'll instruct everyone to give you favourable treatment, on account of your childhood.'

'I'm a little concerned' the master admits to a colleague later that night. 'I've done a recalc on our RS factor, and it seems we're almost full circle.'

'Give us a few years yet' laughs the colleague. 'Anyway, nothing we can do. Whatever will be, will be.'

'And what happened after you let the songbirds out of their cages, Mohammad?'

The Gatekeeper's having a heavy day on the gate, so Christian does the talking.

'They were killed in the yard by hawks. I think it was their fathers' fault.'

'Songbirds do pretty well in cages, don't they. Better than hawks.'

'I reckon the songbirds would have done all right, if only they'd known what to do.'

'They'd have starved to death, Mohammad. By the way, take a look at the eye on this emir. He's going to lose the sight of it. It's a bad sign when the polo gets rough – insurrection brewing. They tell me the viceroy would like to be sultan.'

'He says he'll wait till Barkuk dies.'

'I suppose if Tamerlane can wait, then so can he. But getting back to hawks, they do no good in cages. Like pigeons, they must be free to come and go. We found it the same with our Turkish slaves. You can thank Tamerlane for turning our hawks into songbirds; he wiped out their homeland.'

Christian feels uneasy. The Gatekeeper is too busy to light the hookah, and without Stone conversation with him makes little sense.

'You did no service to those cagebirds letting them out of their cage, Mohammad. It was their fate to be locked up, and you helped them evade their fate.'

'It was their fathers' fault' insists Christian.

'Don't give me *that*! You don't find yourself in a cage for no good reason! Besides, adversity is good for a cagebird, no less than a man. In the manufacture of Our Blessed Stone, the blazing sun produces the best product. Mind you, we don't leave it out in the sun till it frizzles up; that would be bad timing.'

'What *is* Our Stone? And how is it prepared?'

'Sorry, let's speak of pearls and oysters. By taking the dirt from the oyster's shell, you do it no good turn in the long run.'

'You think I did wrong in releasing those birds?'

'No such thing as "wrong" Mohammad: each and every one of us do what we think is right at the time. He who hesitates, we call that "man on the treadmill who won't tread." Truth is not a lake, She is a flowing stream. And did you say you heard the gate speaking?'

'Yes.'

'Good. You see, the Stone doesn't teach you anything: it just helps you realize what you already know.'

'I know' says Christian. 'I just mustn't realize.'

'Oo he's a cunning little minx' says the Gatekeeper to the viceroy. 'He gets through more assass than I'd have thought humanly possible.'

'Let him have his head' says the viceroy. 'What's the word on Miss Living Proof?'

'It seems she was in Baghdad when Tamerlane took the city.'

'Oh.'

Christian sees the Chemical Truth, and feels obliged to record it.

'Sages agree, if the will of man follow Nature, Nature goes beyond the proper point. Sages *also* agree, that in this Work the operator becomes one with his material. Now is the operator part of Nature, or not? If he is, he must go beyond the proper point. If he is not, he is not one with his material.'

Years ahead of its time.

'That silver is found in tin mines, and gold in silver mines, proves only that metals may be converted by Nature from one form to another. It does *not* prove the conversion proceeds towards gold, nor, even if it *did* proceed towards gold, that it necessarily *stops* with gold. Evolution, in the mineral world, proceeds too slowly to be observed. Gold could be made of silver, and silver of tin, for all the evidence proves. But now imagine a *cyclic* process!'

Christian sits back to imagine. All I need are a few facts to pad out my argument, he decides.

'The soul must marry the body, before we can start this Work' says the viceroy.

'I thought that was its aim!'

'The aim of this Work is its precondition.'

'Listen' says Christian, 'can we talk of something else?' He's sick and tired of mathematics. It seems that *all* the numbers from one to ten are sacred and meaningful.

'All right, then: Barkuk's son, Faraj. Raised in a palace!'

Infinity and zero aside, the viceroy is now on his favourite topic. 'Do you mind if I have another smoke?' asks Christian.

'Go ahead. Now poor Faraj, he has no hope of running this empire properly, his sultan father was too busy ever to spend any time with him. That's why I'm not married.'

'You don't have to marry' says Christian.

'It causes trouble if the viceroy's seen in a massage parlour, Mohammad.'

'Do it in secret.'

'What I can't do openly, I never do.'

'Take no notice of what other people think' says Christian. 'That's what the Gatekeeper says.'

'Is that so? Well you tell the Gatekeeper I think he's greedy. Then tell him I've halved his salary. Mind you, he needn't take any notice of what other people think.'

* * *

'You keep the others awake all night with your coughing' complains the master.

'I can't help it' says Christian. 'It's the price I pay to stay normal.'

'So he thinks I'm greedy? The trouble is, Mohammad, what we have in Damascus is the "twilight" system, suitable for empires at their peak, that is, on the way out. The ideas of an empire at its peak, when implemented, bring about its downfall. These are your so-called "enlightened" ideas. What we need to study are the ideas *before* the peak, that lead to that peak when implemented!'

'The fact is' says the master, 'the Gatekeeper covets the viceroy's job, and the viceroy fears industrial action.'

'Another thing' says the viceroy, 'you notice how gatekeepers always bring the conversation round to sex? That's because they're not getting any.'

'I'm not getting any either' says Christian. 'Just lucky I guess.'

'Adultery is hard to avoid in the twilight situation, when the maximum variation is needed to cope with impending crisis.'

'When I was your age' says the Gatekeeper, 'the challenge lay in fucking all the women you could. Today, it's in keeping them out of your pants. Take no notice of the viceroy: he can't get it up.'

'Such foolish ideas lead to impotence' says the master, 'though they call it celibacy.'

'I had a girlfriend once' says Christian. He's forgotten her name already.

* * *

'In the last days of the old empire' cautions the viceroy, 'some strange alliances formed. When last year's conservative finds himself speaking the language of next year's radical, the number is up. And what is this number? Called the "harmonic oscillator," it is written as a sine wave superposed on a cosine. Which brings me to my favorite topic: Barkuk and the way he mismanages this empire!'

'Excuse me' says Christian, 'but I can't do my homework. I haven't the time, brains or energy.'

For homework, he's been told to rewrite a big book, omitting everything involving zero and infinity.

'Barkuk is a very bad sultan indeed! In all the years he's been sultan, he hasn't waged one single war. Of course, the Syrians are happy; this is what they call "stability." In fact, stability requires continual warfare, for economic reasons. Also, deprived of a problem for longer than two generations, you lose the capacity to solve it. Where are you up to in chemistry, by the way?'

'We're just learning to turn lead into gold.'

'I see. It looks as though theory got a little ahead of practice there.'

'May I see you a moment after the meeting' says the viceroy. 'It's about the boy.'

The Gatekeeper grunts. The viceroy has just dismissed a claim on behalf of the gatekeepers.

'We're getting nowhere' says the viceroy. 'It goes in one ear and out the other. He smokes too much. Are you perfectly sure *all* Germans don't have genitals like him?'

'Make it tonight then, if that's how you feel.'

On the evening of the night of the extraordinary smoko, Christian is talking to the Gatekeeper, on the Gatekeeper's last tour of duty before the impending strike.

'It's not when the Rose gives you knowledge, Mohammad, it's when it gives you *power*, you're in trouble.'

'But aren't they the same thing?' This is generally the safest response, Christian has learnt.

'No, of course not. I *prove* I have more knowledge, by my power over the viceroy!'

'The viceroy says he's more powerful, because he knows more than you.'

'Then let him prove it in the next existence. The first part of Our Blessed Work is the killing of the Sun God by his son, who didn't understand a word of what his Dad was saying.'

'I know how he felt' says Christian.

'Staying home tonight Christian?'

The master's caught him at it in his cell. 'Yes' says Christian, 'I thought I'd have a little smoke before I start.'

The master glances at Christian's manuscript: it's rubbish from beginning to end. 'Very well Christian' he says, 'I can see you're determined to force this out of me: the Vegetable Stone is a pharmaceutical warrior! The plants are our brothers, worse luck'.

'I won't turn my back on knowledge' says Christian, exhaling, 'what*ever* its source.'

'Christian' implores the master, 'give up this Black Path. It sends a man to *Hell*!'

'I know' says Christian, 'but what you don't realize, he learns to turn it to his own advantage.'

20

Two thirty a.m., the rosegarden. The Gatekeeper's in a bad mood. 'You go on the gate' he says to Christian, 'I'm going to practice for the strike.'

'It's pretty heavy' says Christian, struggling.

'Have you been doing your push-ups?'

'Yes' says Christian, 'three a day. I didn't want to be hasty.'

'Let's see you close the gate then.'

Closing the gate is easy. It likes to be closed. Once released, it closes with great speed and force, as though of its own accord. Opening the gate is more difficult. The Gatekeeper has to help.

'As long as you can shut the gate' says the Gatekeeper, 'we'll worry about opening it later. You know how Hermes got that caduceus? He once walked into a paralytic ward of the local teaching hospital with a brace of man-eating pythons on his person. Get off your beds and walk, he said. Emptied the place in five seconds flat. It's all in the mind, and what does the mind say? The worst thing that can happen to us is to die a natural death. Eaten by a snake, poisoned by a toadstool.'

'If they were man-eating pythons ...'

'They ate Hermes but spat him out. He wasn't a man anymore. My point is, you could open that gate if your life depended on it. The ultimate gate, Mohammad, is that which awaits us in death. And what does the Grand Gatekeeper say to the latecomer?'

'I know not whence ye are.'

'Correct. So when you hear me shout like thunder, you shut the gate, and what do you say to the latecomer?'

'I know not whence ye are.'

'Correct. There comes a time to die, and one must not survive it.'

The lodge members start arriving shortly afterwards, filing through without speaking. Christian tries to count them, but gives up when two walk through the gate simultaneously.

Suddenly Sal appears, half asleep, ambling slowly down the road.

'Hurry up Sal' shouts Christian. Sal is Christian's best friend.

Thunder claps as Sal is halfway through the iron gate.

'I told you to hurry' says Christian, 'now I know nót whence ye are!'

'Open the gate' screams Sal, 'my leg is caught!'

'I can't' replies Christian. 'My life doesn't depend on it!'

Sal screams, and won't stop screaming. Christian tries to comfort him. 'It's your father's fault' he explains to Sal. 'This wouldn't be happening at all, if you hadn't been such a villain in your previous existence.'

Eventually, Sal falls asleep. 'Wipe that blood off us' says the gate. 'We don't want to become rusty.'

The meeting is rather rowdy, ending early, because of the storm. The Grand Gatekeeper opens the gate, as the viceroy stands and watches.

'It's his father's fault' explains Christian. 'He should have been taught punctuality.'

'He won't walk on *that* leg again' says the viceroy.

'Can you show us what happened?'

'Certainly' says Christian. 'He was standing here, when I heard the thunder.'

The thunder claps again, the gate slams, and Christian feels a dreadful pain. Between his legs.

* * *

'Take that' says the gate. 'Boo, hiss' shout the lodge. 'We know not whence ye are!'

'Don't you care about anyone but yourself?' shout the viceroy and Gatekeeper, in unison. 'Sal's dad may have been a villain, but that was his *gran*dad's fault!'

No use; Christian falls asleep, and while sleeping, has a dream. He's standing on the walls of the city of Damascus, and outside are the Mongols. Next to him stands The One, properly speaking The Two, smiling broadly.

21

Sal is asleep in his hospital bed, with a big smile on his face. The smell from his leg is dreadful, and his bed has collapsed.

'Help' shouts the bed. 'Where've you been? We're in agony here!'

Christian stumbles off to find help. He can't move fast, and feels strange. In fact, he needs a smoke. He finds a doctor on the ground floor. 'I need a smoke' says Christian. He's forgotten about Sal – first things first.

He gets lost on the way back. It's early morning and he's tired. He opens a cupboard, taking it for a door, and finds a stash of the Vegetable Stone.

'Are you discharging yourself *again*?' says the doctor. 'I've looked up your file. You weren't supposed to get any in the first place.'

The Stone is reserved for terminal cases. Christian wastes no time in argument, but staggers off to the polling booth, where viceroy and Grand Gatekeeper stand waiting impatiently on the marble steps. The polling booth is inside the Piebald Palace, and the Gatekeeper has agreed to open the gate. The viceroy is carrying a placard which reads 'Vote for Me and I Won't Have You Executed.' The Gatekeeper is carrying a placard which reads 'Vote for Me and I'll Resign as Executioner.'

Christian has been given the job of pollmaster.

'The votes go in here' says the viceroy, tapping a barrel. 'No one must cast two votes.'

Oh well, thinks Christian, sitting behind the barrel, with any luck there'll be a slack turnout.

The viceroy and Gatekeeper run off in different directions: voting is not compulsory.

'Have you seen our girlfriend?' says the bottom of the barrel. 'My word, she's a little charmer. We refer to our copper fittings. Chuck us one down, why don't you.'

Christian has a dream. His father stands in the backyard, close to the pines. The air is cool and moist. A cold toad suckles the breast of a woman. Once in a while the toad belches. 'Now listen' says the count, 'if you don't wake up to yourself, son, I'll throw you in the nether regions, bolted by iron gates and a copper threshold.' He takes a run-up, and a gold chain hurtles down the slope from his hand. The toad starts, then resumes suckling. It's now bigger than the woman.

Wake up! It's the Gatekeeper and the viceroy back. Night has fallen already. 'You have to watch us count the votes' they say, 'and make sure we don't cheat.' Eagerly, they unlock the barrel, only to find it empty.

Neither guru is keen to proceed, as the pollmaster casts the decider.

'We'll have to abide by the rules' says the viceroy, 'at least till we see the outcome. Mohammad, you go to bed, sort yourself out, we'll see you tomorrow.'

'And no Stone' adds the Gatekeeper.

'That's right' says the viceroy, 'absolutely none!'

'Now wait a minute' says Christian, 'I can live without it, but prefer not to!'

'Learn to know when you've had enough!'

I've had enough, learns Christian. I'm getting out of this city. I don't want to know what's right or wrong, I just want to get right out of it.

'You're cooking with the gas now' says the bottom of the barrel.

He gets as far as the hospital, then suffers the familiar feeling of having left something behind him. Retracing his steps, he overhears the viceroy discussing his progress.

'Yes, no doubt our most advanced student. However, and this is critical . . .'

'There we are' says the bottom of the barrel. 'What'd we tell you, Mohammad? You're the most advanced student, now don't wait round to hear more.'

'I won't ' says Christian. 'It's true, it must be. It's the only thing they agree on.'

'Why not take us with you' says the iron-bottomed barrel with the copper fittings. 'We can be of use. First go back to hospital. Now take all that hospital Stone, for safekeeping.'

'Good idea' says Christian. 'What I can't sell, I can smoke.'

He fills the barrel with Vegetable Stone, and rolls it out the gate at sunrise. The city gate is open, and because of the strike, unattended.

22

'God save thee, stranger! If thou hast heard anything concerning the nuptials of the King, consider these words. By us doth the Bridegroom offer thee a choice between foure ways, all of which, if thou dost not sink down in the way, can bring thee to his royal court. The first is short but dangerous, and one which will lead thee into rocky places, through which it will scarcely be possible to pass. The second is longer, and takes thee circuitously; it is plain and easy, if by the help of the Magnet, thou turnest neither to left nor right. The third is that truly royal way which through various pleasures and pageants of our King, affords thee a joyful journey; but this so far has scarcely been allotted to one in a thousand. By the fourth shall no man reach the place, because it is a consuming way, practicable only for incorruptible bodies. Choose now which thou wilt, and persevere constantly therein; for know whichsoever thou shalt enter, that is the one destined for thee by immutable Fate, nor canst thou go back therein save at great peril to life!'

The Chymical Marriage

'It's no good me just *nibbling* this stuff' explains Christian to the barrel. 'If I'm to experience the so-called mental effect, I'll need a large dose.'

The barrel, well aware that Christian experiences the so-called mental effect most days, expresses reservations.

'Maybe it's just your short-term memory is playing up on you, boss. Besides, you're going to be so wise, it won't be funny.'

'I know' says Christian, 'that's a risk we have to take. I can't push this loaded barrel two feet further, I'm going to eat half.'

Forty days later, a traveller reports seeing a pillar of salt, sitting on a barrel pointed at Damascus, near the old fort at Kerak. This pillar is in fact Christian, who has completely dissolved and recrystallized. It would take a larger library than the one in Alexandria to record what he's been through, and we shan't attempt it here; but fortunately, we have no need, for the whole Mystery of the Cosmos – the Crux of the Gnosis – the Essence of Vegetable Wisdom – is etched, in a single phrase, indelibly on Christian's cortex, and it came about in the following way:

At one point on his inward journey, Christian found himself in a castle, immured with a number of magi like himself. At midnight, he's woken by his page, and escorted into the castle's bowels, down a long, winding, clammy flight of stairs. Christian, naturally, is excited, and full of questions about the castle. As castles go, it's the finest he's seen.

'It belonged to the Assassins' explains his page. 'A feature of the design, the dungeon we're about to visit represents the lowest point in the cosmos.'

The steps wind down, till eventually the path of the lads is blocked by a huge door, with certain strange, copper letters fixed to it.

'Can you make out the language?' asks Christian.

'It translates "The Highest Medicine is found in the Poisonous Dragon," but the idea's to concentrate on substance, not style. That is, the fact these words are made of copper, is more important than what they actually say.'

The door is opened, and the page leads Christian by the hand through a very dark passage, till they come to a little door only recently closed. As the page informs Christian, this was first opened when the coffins (for the King and his Bridal

Party) were removed.

'This is what I call a castle' says Christian, inside the vault. The vault contains no other light, but that from certain carbuncles.

'This is the Treasury' explains the page. 'Its principal feature is the sepulchre. You'll note it's triangular, contains a copper kettle, but is otherwise of gold and precious stones.'

'Charming' says Christian. 'The question is, how come no one's guarding it?'

The page shrugs and Christian hobbles across for a closer view. In the kettle stands an angel, who holds in his arms an unknown tree. Around the tree are little fires. The fruit from the tree is continually melting and falling into the kettle, where it turns into water, and runs out into three small golden kettles nearby. The altar is supported by an eagle, an ox, a lion and a naked lady.

'Shall we drink a little?' asks Christian. 'It's my policy to try everything a few times.'

'I don't think we should drink it' says the page. 'But I guess a little *sniff* could do no harm.'

They each take a sniff, and straightway the page points to a copper door in the floor.

'Down we go' he says. 'There's no stopping till you reach rock bottom, and this is it!'

'I think I'll give it a miss' says Christian. 'I don't feel good, and hopooid vodgrais lpbs epgraoooob oosfxsg.'

'Gpdsxogh bxgg' laughs the page, and down they go.

'OXO BSPFSUCHG! OPSOPE DXOOS OSSG VOGGPOBB, UPSBCHOPSFPOMPSB!'

'Sch xufwxchpo' replies the page. 'Vob pjo ougps, bpjo psopb bopbopalui. And now we better get out of here.'

Just as they're leaving the vault, in comes Cupid the dwarf. At first he's suspicious, but seeing the lads frightened, more dead than alive, he starts laughing.

'He lost his way' explains the page, 'and I was just helping him out.'

'OXO BSPFSUCHG' says Christian, excitedly. 'OPSOPE DXOOS OSSG VOGGPOBB, UPSBCHOPSFPOMPSPB!'

'I can't let it pass so easily' says Cupid. 'You nearly stumbled on my dead mother Venus!'

He fixes a lock on the door in the floor, and strikes a dart from his quiver in one of the little fires that force the tree in the kettle to melt.

'When that tree is melted down' he says, pricking Christian in the hand, 'then shall Venus awake and give birth to a new King. In the meantime, Robbers of the Rosegarden out of here. Or do you want what you really want? Wait a minute. I see from your codpiece you got what you really wanted!'

'I wonder what he meant by that exactly' says Christian, back in his bedroom. It's a funny thing, but when you get what you really want, you forget you wanted it.

From the road Hebron is a cluster of flat-roofed houses of mud and stone, on the slopes of a hill surmounted by an olive grove. Some of the houses have grass growing on their roofs. There are plenty of vacant lots, or walled gardens you could call them, except the walls are falling down, and the gardens consist of eroded dirt, rubble stone, dusty trees and household garbage. Many of the houses are two-storied, and half way up the hill is a large wall surrounding what looks like a monastery. There aren't many people about, apart from the occasional porter with his filthy beard, and here and there a child lying under a wall.

Christian stops at David's Pool, a sort of open-air Turkish bath filled with floating ordure, to quench his thirst. The usual street boys, dressed in pyjamas, materialize from nowhere at the sight of so distinguished a stranger, and start demanding money.

'Oxo bspfsuchg' explains Christian. 'Opsope dxoos ossg voggpobb, upsbchopsfpompspb.'

Betray the Mysteries? It's not so easy. The boys, in pity, donate a sum sufficient for Christian to book into the local inn. The accommodation isn't much, a barn, with platforms running round the walls, men on the platforms, animals on the floor, a manger for first-class travellers. But next to the inn stands a little wine bar, and Christian, possessed of his magic formula, wanders over, pushing his barrel, to commence the Reformation of the Whole Wide World.

There's only one other drinker there, a small, red-headed man.

The bar's a shambles. Stepping over stools and fixtures, Christian orders a drink.

'A bottle of the Real Thing' he says, 'the Drink that makes you Thirsty.'

'Hi there' says the red-headed man, producing a sacred book. 'Friend, I can see from your face you're lost, and are wondering what life's all about.'

'On the contrary' protests Christian, '*you're* the one who's lost! Oxo bspfsuchg! Opsope dxoos ossg voggpobb upsbchopsfpompspb!'

'Please boys' implores the publican, 'can't you go elsewhere? You Sons of the Sun have frightened off all my regular clientele!'

It's a nightmare, constipation apart. Everywhere Christian goes, he meets with would-bes if they could-bes in their droves. Entering a bar anywhere, is like entering a mirror. Would-be if they could-be Sons of the Sun, babbling on every corner.

'*I* have the Truth' shouts Christian, time and again. 'You only *think* you do! Oxo bspfsuchg, opsope dxoos ossg voggpobb, upsbchopsfpompsb!'

'And what are *you* supposed to represent?' says a heavy-jowled Jew in Jerusalem. Christian and half a dozen would-bes if they could-bes are vying for his attention.

'I don't know' answers Christian truthfully. 'They don't tell us that.'

'Maybe you're a horseman of the Apocalypse. You're not the

first horseman though, you know why?'

'No. Why?'

'It's his job to slice the vaginal sphincter. That's why dildoes and arseholes are the rage today.'

'Listen' says Christian, 'you seem intelligent . . .'

'Thank you' says the man, laughing.

'Seriously, I've something may help you understand what I'm trying to say.'

'All right, just this once I'll do it. Why should I miss out on all the fun?'

A few hours later the man is enlightened, but at what cost to Christian! Of his original stash of Stone, barely one quarter remains.

'Amazing' says the Jew, shaking his head in disbelief. 'Oxus beefsteak, who would have thought it? Opsoap winebar dopehead downo, if upjack arsetit pompchat wishbone. I gotta go straight off and warn my colleagues!'

He leaves Christian on the horns of a dilemma: the Reformation of the Whole Wide World requires an infinite quantity of Stone, it seems, and Christian himself gets through a fair bit, notwithstanding chronic constipation. What to do? He has the Tincture, but without the Mercury, can't make more.

Walking to the window of the rented room, he looks out over the city. Seeing Tancred's Tower, he thinks of Pal, and is filled with indignation.

'Moslems, Jews and Christians' he shouts, 'will ye none of ye heed ye me? What must I do to convince this corrupt world I have seen The Truth?'

'Well, for a start' says a passing Arab, 'you could do something about that appearance. Nervous tremor, hacking cough, pasty face, pigeon chest, squeeky voice – you'd be the world's ugliest adolescent. Who's going to listen to you?'

'Listen' says Christian, 'I had a virile member two feet long!'

'Oh. What happened to it?' A crowd's gathered, come to enjoy the fun.

'It got caught in a gate.'

* * *

There's no one I can turn to for advice, thinks Christian, no one but me knows anything. But wait on; what about that man in Fez who can see into the future? No one can tell me what to do, but if someone could tell me what I end up doing, I guess that would be of help.

At the foot of the stairs he finds his sole initiate, the merchant Jew.

'Hey listen Pal, three queries: one, it seems we need that Stone to see what Moses saw without it, so what can we see without it he needed it to see; two, am I right in thinking the first part of this Work is in spreading the bullshit everywhere, followed by the weeding-out of the unlooked-for consequences; three, I hope ten minutes a day will be enough, it's all the time I can spare.'

23

The bazaar in Fez is very crowded with its usual conglomerate of Berbers, Florentines, Genoese, Venetians, Egyptians, Syrians and Nubians. Christian enters a small magic shop and rings the bell on the counter. An old shop assistant comes out from behind a display of mummified monkeys' paws.

'Hello' he says, 'can I interest you in a farting cushion?'

'No thank you' says Christian, 'I seek the man who can see into the future.'

'Here we are' says the shop assistant, 'just come in from China. Stochastic cards, guaranteed meaningless. Five hundred denars the deck.'

'Look I'm sorry, I'm afraid I . . .'

'Deck of Tarot cards, guaranteed meaningful? Five hundred denars?'

'Look, I'm very sorry . . .'

'All right then, something just for fun. Doggy Done It, for the mosque.'

The Grand Prognosticator sits in a booth at the far end of the shop, restrained by ethics from charging admission or advertising in the press. Correctly surmising a small purchase at the counter will help defray costs, Christian, armed with a bottle of bullshit repellent, enters the booth.

The GP takes one look at him, then searches the crystal ball.

'Son of a miner' he pronounces.

'Wrong' says Christian, 'son of a count.'

'Here you are, entering a German school to study law.'

'Law' says Christian, amazed. 'How old am I?'

'Younger than you are now. I hope it's been explained to you I deal only with the future? What I see here before me is your next existence.'

'Oh that's no good to me' explains Christian. 'Can't you confine yourself to this one?'

'You can easily extrapolate back, using the Law of Karma. I'm getting some really incredibly bad vibes here, you know. The ball's gone foggy.'

'I don't think I want to hear more' says Christian. 'Have you a toilet?'

'The ball is clearing. You've entered a monastery.'

'Oh no . . .'

'Here you are fasting and praying, but nothing seems to go right. Look at this, you're cursing the Pope! Blaming the system for your constipation! And now you're nailing some sort of crapulous document to a door.'

'Oh really, how trivial . . .'

'No! Don't ask me why, but this must be a momentous occasion. I've never seen my crystal ball quiver like this before. Hang on, if I peer closely, I can just make out your name . . .'

The Grand Prognosticator fastens his face to the ball, which is glowing and growling.

'Let me see now . . . Muddy Waters? No.'

Sprock! A great crack ruptures the ball, splitting it down one side.

'Monty Christo? No.'

'Listen' says Christian, 'if I were you . . .'

'Got it! MARTIN LUTHER!'

The crystal ball, with a crack like thunder, explodes, showering the booth with glass. Christian, deafened by the screaming of his *vis-à-vis,* stumbles blindly out.

* * *

Phew. What a shocking, profitless experience, he thinks to himself later. Still, it helped me make a decision: I won't attempt, any longer, the Reformation of the Whole Wide World. These infidels are too far gone. Besides, they heard what I had to say, and chose to ignore it.

No, I'm going to concentrate on Germany, my Fatherland. Germany, my Fatherland – your Christian is coming home!

*R*eturn of Christian Rosy Cross

Resumé

Brother R.C. departed the city Fez, and sailed with many costly things into Spain, hoping well, as he himself had so well and profitably spent his time in his travel, that the learned in Europe would highly rejoyce with him, and begin to rule and order all their studies according to those sure and sound foundations . . .

Fama Fraternitatis

24

Christian is arrested by the Inquisition shortly after leaving Granada, a Moslem strip stuck like a plaster on the open sore of Christendom. He tries to defend himself, but is forced to silence by the quotation of certain remarks made in the course of his last public lecture, by a man he clearly recalls as having been the only member of the audience.

'And where did the money for the hall hire come from?' demands the Inquisitor, thumping the dock. 'If it can be shown he *sold* this concoction, I demand the maximum penalty!'

Christian, though prepared to give away what he can't consume, and to sell what he can't give away, is on firm ground here.

'I can't sell what was *stolen*' he protests. 'I accuse this man of theft! He's the only person in the whole of Europe who could have known the value of my Stone.'

'We're not here to listen to *your* accusations, we've heard enough of those. Take him away!'

Christian is cast in the deepest dungeon at the Pope's palace in Avignon. His surmise that some of his Vegetable Stone has preceded him there is correct. Decimated by the spy, it stands on a plate in a cell by itself, with several distinguished scholars debating its composition full-time. As direct determination of its efficacy is deemed dangerous, it is subjected instead to all manner of chemical analysis, using the most modern techniques. It is fused; ignited; made into cement; incinerated; exposed to corrosive vapour; mixed with solvents; and when after seven years of tests its composition remains unclear, the Pope give guarded approval for its trial on a human subject. A young nun from a closed order is given a piece to eat. When nothing happens, Christian, who all this time has languished in his cell, is pronounced a nuisance, and left to remain, rotting where he is, for the term of his natural life.

The year is 1401 and Christian is twenty-three years old.

He's had a lot to think about in the past seven years, and if he knew the stories that have grown around his name, and the miracles wrought in that name by the Stone (multiplied, by wishful thinking, many times), he'd have even more. A new generation of heretics find their inspiration in Christian. The Pope, though well aware of this development, has sense enough not to make him a martyr, and prefers to keep him, with all Millenarians and other nuisances, out of the way.

Christian, while confined to himself, is not entirely cut off from the world, and often gets to hear of current affairs through the guards.

'You was in Damascus wasn't you guv? Thought you was. 'Eard last night the place is 'istory! Not a stone left standing. Nasty lot them Mongols, you gotta 'and it to 'em. You know in all the time them Mongols been fightin', they never give a prisoner yet? Always fight to the deaf. Well, I mean to say, they may as well be monsters. 'Ope they never get over 'ere.'

'What's that Harry? Damascus sacked?'

'So I 'eard, guv. Mind you, could be wrong.'

'Find out Harry. Can you get the details? Harry, this is *most important*!'

'All right, see what I can do. 'Appen you'll do me a favour one day.'

Since the book on which he's been working for the past five years is now defunct, it's with unmixed feelings Christian listens to Harry's further details.

'Seems it's right guv. Nasty business. Infidels opened the gate and let them in.'

'What! Oh Harry, I can't believe *that,* I know the gatekeeper, he'd never do it!'

' 'Appen. 'e was under orders guv. 'Ey, 'ow about this for a larf: Tamerlane stood outside the gate, swore on the Koran 'e'd do no 'arm!'

'And they believed him.'

'Yeah, but you gotta understand their mentality. Accordin' to them, if you swear on the Koran you won't do somethin' then go a'ead and do it, you're in the poo. But Tamerlane, 'e don't give a fuck about religion, all 'e wants is to get in that gate! You feelin' all right guv?'

'I can't believe that anyone could do such an evil thing.'

'*Evil*! Nuffin' evil about it, dead clever, that's what it was. Any'ow, you're an 'eretic, what's evil to you?'

'And the Damascans?'

'You know what those Mongols are like guv: torture's their idea o' sport.'

'God Harry, I *knew* those people!'

'And I understand 'ow you feel. But there's a *lesson* for the likes of you and me in the fate o' that city, and it's this: never believe your own bullshit to the point where you think everyone else does!'

'Harry, will you do me a favour? Tell the Pope I want to recant. The second part of this Work is the undoing of the first, if at all possible.'

The following morning Pope Benedict XIII of Avignon grants Christian an audience. Christian, with a winding sheet under his arm in the manner of a Mameluke penitent traitor, expresses regret at having destroyed Christendom, ascribing his behaviour to bad karma acquired in the course of previous existences.

'We don't believe in reincarnation' says the Pope. 'Believe that, and you'll believe anything. It's the ultimate existentialist fantasy.'

'It keeps the peasant in his place' protests Christian.

'Perhaps, but I won't stoop so low. I admit there were founding fathers of the Church who took the doctrine seriously, Origen for one. He made himself a eunuch. Anyhow, there's not a shred of evidence. Let me put it this way: the ultimate test of a theory is *not,* does it account for the facts?, but is it True? Reincarnation may well account for the facts, but is it True? We're only born once, it says that in the Bible. We're only born once and we only die once, but villains, who for obvious reasons can't accept the dogma of eternal Hell, propose these alternatives. Can you recall your previous existence?'

'No' says Christian, 'but I blame myself.'

'Oh you blame yourself, do you? You don't blame yourself for the evil you've done, but you blame yourself for not being able to recall something that happened before you were born. What's the matter with you?'

'Listen' says Christian, 'I came here to be forgiven, not criticized! Are you going to forgive me, or do I go to Rome and confess to the opposition?'

'Forgive you! After what you've done!'

'If I'm big enough to admit I was wrong, can I get off the hook by spreading the word?'

'That's what you *all* say' says the Pope. 'Tell you what though, see this pastoral staff? If it bursts into bud in the next three days, you're a free man. I'll let you go.'

I've no right to mercy, thinks Christian in his cell. Still, you have to break rules sometimes. We wouldn't have one pope today, let alone two, if Paul hadn't disregarded Christ's rule not to take His teaching to the gentiles.

The Pope consults his most trusted adviser and master of the Preacher's Order.

'I'm completely opposed to it' says the preacher. 'I thought we discussed this before. The only authorities on matters like the Stone are those who *don't* know what they're talking about.

Those who *do* know what they're talking about are either zealous crusaders or paranoic apostates, and this chap has simply gone from one to the other category. The Stone doesn't care if you love it or hate it, provided you talk about it all the time.'

'Yes, but the situation is desperate. I must try something new.'

'Something *new!*'

'I'm sorry, I didn't mean that. I'm under dreadful strain. We're losing the battle to heresy, it's completely out of hand.'

'I think you should burn him, as an example.'

'We, as Christians of all people, should understand the power of martyrdom. The Rosicrucians will go berserk! They're bad enough now!'

'Burn them as well.'

'My dear fellow, it's been tried again and again, and it doesn't work. What is needed is a bold, imaginative stroke of policy from me.'

'My God: you're *not* going to make him a saint and give him his own order!'

'I wouldn't have the nerve for that. And when Innocent III took Francis in, don't forget he used Dominic as counter-weight. I'm wondering what impact he might not have with his own cult, don't you see? He'll be an embarrassment to them, at the very least. Of course, he'll need re-educating, but he seems keen.'

'I think you're making a grave error.'

When the Pope next day visits the dungeons, he overhears Christian reading.

'Rome in its last days, Harry, suffered severe lead poisoning. The people, in desperate search for gold, whored with foreign gods. Men were abandoning Bacchus for Christ, and Jupiter for Osiris. And Who, in each case, Harry, mediated this switch? Who is He Who helps man slip from one set of rules to another? Who can teach the power of knowing both sets of rules at once? Hermes. For just as serpent sloughs his skin, so man must emerge from outmoded Law, when that Law no longer guarantees him freedom, justice or truth. The Son must slay the Father in this Work! The Stone must be black before it is white! Hermes guides us through the darkness of rebellion, to the white light of the New Law.'

'As you say, guv.'

Christian dashes his book to the floor.

'But Harry, don't you see, it's all *wrong*! Look at Rome, look at Damascus! Societies perish as a result of this individual, uncoordinated freedom. A society enlightened enough to hate war, is conquered by another less enlightened! I didn't understand what my master meant, when he said it was fatal for Turks to love Truth.'

'But now you do, eh guv?'

'Do I ever! Hermes, if He can't convert us all, destroys us, and how many understand what He says?'

'I'll take over thanks, Harry' says the pontiff, stepping delighted from the dark. 'What I've heard fully convinces me this is the man for the job, and look!'

He holds aloft his pastoral staff, a droopy leaf stuck to it.

'*I* can't make 'ead nor tail o' what 'e says, your 'oliness.'

'Neither can I! You see, Harry, we need a new kind of preacher in our Church today. We old fellows have lost touch. But here is a man who both speaks the language of the young and repudiates their values. Christian, it's true, is it not, you no longer worship Hermes?'

'The god of the few must be sacrificed to the god of the many' says Christian, darkly.

'And you don't mind staying in Europe?'

'On the contrary, I'm encouraged by the materialism here. The Vegetable Stone will never replace the Mineral Stone in Europe. Men hungry for gold presumably feel that gold buys something of value. It's all very heartening. Who knows, I may yet wind up with that castle I always craved.'

'Oh look' says Harry, cleaning out the cell. 'He left 'is book be'ind 'im. Seems a shame to burn it, after all that work put in.'

25

Christian is ordained by the Pope himself; quite an honour.

'You realize I shouldn't be doing this' says the pontiff. 'I'm stretching the rules.'

'Please' says Christian, 'no more talk of the Stone, if you knew how it hurt! I must begin the second phase of the Work, undoing the first.'

'It's not that' says the Pope, 'it's your penis: it's supposed to be in one piece.'

After ordination, the Pope invites Christian back to the palace for tea. Just wait till Boniface hears about *this*, the pontiff thinks to himself.

Boniface IX is the Roman Pope, supported by England, Hungary, Bohemia, Portugal and half of Italy, with the rest of Europe supporting Benedict. There will be two popes, until in 1409 the Council of Pisa elects Alexander V. Then, for a while, there'll be three.

Christian, in his fresh white Dominican habit, proposes a toast to himself.

'Bet you never thought you'd finish up a priest' says the Pope.

'I haven't finished up yet.'

The master of Christian's order, however, makes plain his own feelings next day.

'If it were up to me' he says, 'you'd be burnt at the stake.'

'I deserve it too' says Christian. 'As society breaks down, mutants develop, lacking all social conscience. In the short term, this confers on them an advantage over their celebate fellows. Let's analyse the development of this situation.'

'Some other time' says the preacher.

'I believe Francis responsible for our problems. Dominic saw it, but was powerless to intervene.'

'Don't you dare talk like that' says the preacher. 'We must maintain unity! Why only last night, one of my friends, an Augustinian friar . . . '

'Augustine' sneers Christian, 'ex-gnostic, self-confessed!'

The Pope happens by, and listens, amazed at the extent of Christian's conversion.

'What's *wrong* with us?' demands Christian. 'Have we confused charity with duty? What's wrong with our immune system we can't annihilate tumours?'

'It's a question of identification' says the Pope. 'We can't always pick 'em.'

'*I* can pick 'em' says Christian, 'and do you know *how* I pick'em?'

'No' says the preacher, 'and I shouldn't have thought it's a matter you'd wish to dwell on. It seems as though I'm stuck with you, so I'm sending you off with some experienced men in the morning, in the hope you'll learn by example.'

'Let me at 'em' says Christian, grinning. The Pope smiles weakly and the preacher goes red.

I wonder how *they* got the cardinal's hat, thinks Christian, back in his room. They don't know much. Poor old Dominic, *he* saw the Secret of the Stone, but got the crooked end of the crosier. I've heard him called unchristian by those tumourphile Franciscans. Can't they see the outer circle must protect the inner? Did Christ, Who was all charity, show charity to Pharisees? Where would the Church be today, if we only practised what we always preach? Oh no, there's no greater error than thinking Moses wrong because Christ was right. The Founding Fathers were wiser than we. So the latest word is the Devil must have His day is it? We'll see about that! *My* vision of the Reformation of the World has the Wolf lying down with the Lamb.

No use the Wolf lying down if the Lamb won't come to the party, Christian. The Secret of the Stone leaves two modes of action open to those who know it.

26

The Inquisition prepares to depart. Along with Christian and his personal boy, Adam Cadman, are three Dominican friars. Ancillary staff – servants, cooks, cellarmen – come to a dozen or more. They're a crack unit, the flying squad; hand-picked by the Pope.

They ride away, by papal dispensation: mendicant monks are supposed to walk. Christian, suitably grim, rides in front. On the outskirts of Avignon, they're joined by some knights.

'Tell me O'Reilly, where is heresy found?'

'It is found, Brother Christian, wherever you choose to look. It is found in the cities, it is found in the towns. It is found among the rich, it is found among the poor. It is found among the young, it is found among the old. It is found among the clergy . . .'

'I get the picture' says Christian. 'It is within those moving and those standing still. It is the knowledge which leads its master away from the misery of the world, and back to the knowledge of good things to come. In other words, the Vegetable Stone.'

'Don't be hasty, Brother Christian. You can be an heretic without the Vegetable Stone.'

'Bullshit' snaps Christian. 'Believe that, you'll believe anything!'

* * *

'I think I'll stroll through the village before I retire, Adam' says Christian that night.

'Shouldn't you take a knight for protection?'

'When the king had drunk from the waters, Adam, he became ill but later regained his health. What does a healthy man have to fear from an ill one?'

'Illness?'

'I'm speaking as a healthy man, Adam, not an ordinary one. Don't you know the difference?'

'Evidently not.'

'The healthy man has *recovered* from his illness. This makes him immune.'

'But father, there's more than one kind of illness!'

'Bullshit, Adam! Believe that, you'll believe anything!'

'You're sure we're not making a mistake?' says O'Reilly, later that night. 'They seem nice young people. No duenna, but no shilly shally, and not a drop of liquor in the house.'

'Two more counts in the indictment' says Christian.

An older man, obviously the master in heresy, smiles at Christian as the knights lead him off. 'Pax, young master. We all freak out. Don't get uptight. You need the right surroundings.'

'Shut up' says Christian. 'You make me sound old-fashioned, and I'm years ahead of my time.'

The trial is held in the local hall. 'About this Vegetable Stone' says Christian.

'Is *that* what you call it?' says the culprit. 'Anyway, it's not against the law.'

'He's right' says the notary, wearily. 'It's not against the law.'

'Case adjourned!'

'How can I conduct an Inquisition' says Christian, 'when the worst sin in the Book is not against the law?'

'For one thing' says the notary, 'it's not in the Book, and if it were, there'd be worse sins than taking a puff or two of a harmless liquor substitute. You should get your priorities straight.'

That night Christian rides back to Avignon and interrupts the Pope's midnight audience.

'The worst sin's not in the Book' he protests. 'Do something at once!'

'What are you saying?'

'The Vegetable Stone is not against the law! As a matter of fact, it's not in the Book. So either promulgate a new law, or write a new Book.'

'Have a glass of '99' says the Pope. 'I can't write a new Book, but there's no need for that; the Book has been so designed, you can read into it anything you want, which has its drawbacks, as well as its disadvantages. As to promulgating a new law, don't you realize anything against the law is ten times more attractive?'

'Of course' says Christian, 'I wasn't born yesterday! So all we can do is reinterpret the Book. Very well, that Tree of Knowledge – make it a Vegetable Stone.'

'I can't do that' says the Pope. 'That would be spelling things out. Were I so much as to acknowledge its existence, that would be a concession. Wasn't it you who said to me, *we* must dictate the terms of the battle?'

'Yes, but put yourself in my position. How can I fight something I daren't mention, that's not in the Book, that's not against the law, and I can't show people without hurting them?'

'Well you're the man with all the answers. You tell me.'

There *must* be a solution, thinks Christian as he rides back to camp. I'll speak to the culprit in camera.

'I know you're a villain. That's why I'm here. Why not confess?'
'My conscience is clear. I've done nothing wrong.'

'I can get nasty. Confess or else!'
'Confess what, and or else what?'
'Never you mind!'
'I'm not afraid of physical pain.'
'I'll take away your Vegetable Stone!'
'I can live without it.'
'Ha' laughs Christian. 'Gotcha! Once you've tried it, you can *never* live without it!'

'How much longer?' complains the notary. Got to be moving on.'
'I know – one more week should do it. He'll crack, you watch him.'
'Best put the screws on. It's the only way. Unpack the rack. Get O'Hara to write the confession. Stop wasting time!'
Morale is low. Christian, promoted by papal whim, has bungled his first job.
'If he can't extract a confession here' say the knights, 'how will he go in Bohemia?'

'I think we should let him go' says O'Reilly. 'Look at this splendid belt he's made me.'
'I'll give you a tip' says O'Hara. 'Don't arrest if you can't convict. It puts the Church in a poor light.'
The Pope himself is not safe from O'Hara, and that's one reason O'Hara's on the road.
How does he do it, thinks Christian. An iron man! Two weeks and *still* no ill effects!

The man's released, for lack of evidence. 'Ah Christian' says O'Reilly, 'you can't blame the lad. The craft guilds are collapsing. A journeyman today has little chance of owning his business. It breeds discontent.'

* * *

At O'Hara's insistence, things are done correctly in Navarre, beginning with a sermon against heresy.

'No, let Brother O'Reilly do it' says O'Hara, pushing Christian from the pulpit.

During the short time of grace permitted, no one turns himself in, and it's now the duty of the faithful to identify the heretics.

'Here's where you must be careful, Christian. There's always a certain amount of ill-will, and you can't believe all you hear.'

'How do you know what to believe?' asks Adam.

'You trust in the Blessed Virgin. Now go and help unpack the ropes and pulleys, we may be needing those.'

'The good of the few' explains Christian to Adam, 'must bow to the good of the many. Personally, I was well on the way to Heaven worshipping Hermes, and it wasn't until I saw Him sending others to Hell, I thought twice. The Church is the Way of the Magnet, if you like; slower, but more reliable.'

'There's a group of people living on a farm near here, who haven't been to church in six months. Interestingly, they're all graduates, and you know what they raise on that farm? Shetland ponies and Old English Sheep Dogs.'

'Right' says O'Hara, 'move in! I went to university myself!'

I didn't even go to school, thinks Christian. What could I have done, given the chance?

'They claim they're productive members of society, but I think they're referring to a cough.'

'You must satisfy yourself as to guilt or innocence' says O'Hara. 'You're the Inquisitor.'

'Guilty' says Christian.

'No' says O'Reilly, 'they must make free confession.'

'Threaten them with torture' explains O'Hara. 'I recommend strappado. We're not allowed to threaten life or limb, so we threaten joint and ligament.'

'I want these lads to experience a *natural* high' says Christian. 'Then they'll gladly abjure. Guards! Take the defendants, and give them a hot bath, followed by a cold bath.

'I had one myself last night. It made me feel grouse.'

27

'I don't understand' says Christian. 'I can only assume the hot bath was too hot, or the cold bath too cold.'

'There'll be hell to pay over this' fumes O'Hara. I told you not to threaten life or limb!'

'But Adam and I did the very same thing' says Christian, 'and all we felt was exhilaration!'

'We'd better be moving on' says O'Hara. 'We've our reputation to race.'

'I shouldn't be surprised if Navarre goes Roman now' says O'Hara, mounting up.

'Oh leave off' says O'Reilly. 'Christian wasn't to know his tonic would act as a poison!'

'A shmall doshe of poishon ish what a tonic ish' says the notary, swaying from side to side.

'Speaking of poison' says Christian, 'where in hell are they getting all this Stone?'

Close to the border with hot, dry Castile they encounter their first Rosicrucians. The court is crowded, largely with scholars come to witness the confrontation.

'Boo hiss' shout the people. 'Boiled a group of farmers then threw them in the snow to freeze!'

'Silence in the court' orders Christian. 'Now then, who's the first defendant?'

A red-headed man steps forward with alacrity. 'Watch him' warns O'Hara, 'he turned himself in. He means to nail you.'

'*I* should worry' laughs Christian. 'All he knows, he got from me. Now then fellow, what of this Art?'

'You're living proof' says the man.

'That is no secret' admits Christian. 'However, when I found I was buying insight at the expense of my power to enact what I'd learnt . . .'

'You lost nerve. You backtracked.'

Cheers at this, from the defendants.

'The fact is' continues the redhead, 'Our Blessed Stone lost faith in *you*!'

'On the contrary' replies Christian, 'I lost faith in *it*.'

Laughter from the defendants. O'Hara squirms.

'Observe' says the redhead, appealing to the mob, 'this dog of the Lord before us, was once *the* Christian Rosy Cross, author of Our Noble Book.'

Mutterings.

'*Do* something' hisses O'Hara. 'He's gaining the upper hand!'

Christian, white as a sheet, gulps water. 'What book was that' he inquires.

'How to Do It and Get It.'

'By One who Did It and Got It?'

'Of course.'

'Did you write that book, Christian?' asks O'Hara.

'I may have done' says Christian, 'but it's all wrong, you see. I left instructions for it to be destroyed.'

The redhead raises two fingers in the air and starts to quote from the book.

' "From an ass to a philospher and back to an ass, with the aid of the Virgin's Milk: in these words, Sons, do we designate St Albert, known to us as Albertus Magnus, author of the *Little Albert*, a magical treatise unparalleled, yet written by a Christian saint. For he who knows not when to remove his vessel from the hotplate . . ." '

'Rubbish' shouts O'Hara, jumping to his feet. 'Surely we must realize Albert didn't write *half* the works that appear in his noble name!'

'See what happens when you don't take the pot off the stove?' warns the redhead. 'You don't need a new *pot*, you need a new *stove*!'

'Alchemists' continues O'Hara, 'to lend their miserable works authority, frequently publish them under the name of a saint, or Greek philosopher. Why only last year I condemned a man who'd been writing in the name of Thomas Aquinas. He claimed he was a reborn version of the saint. Straight up and down, he was; weighed about five stone.'

'Please' begs Christian. 'The Stone is a net, cast by the Devil, to trap and confound!'

'Then how come in the Great Book you called it a Mystery, Given of God?'

'Here' says O'Hara, 'I knew I had it: a list of the works of Raymond Lully: 7 on rhetoric, 22 on logic, 7 on understanding, 32 on physics, 26 on metaphysics, 212, that's 212 mind you, on theology . . .'

'Two hundred and thirteen' says a voice.

'Sixty on the *Ars Veritas Demonstrativus* . . .'

'Deny you wrote that book' roars the redhead.

'It's true the Arabs gave me the *Ars*' says Christian, 'but I'm the Inquisitor. I have the numbers, that's what's important. It's all in the *numbers*, you fool!'

'This man' says the redhead, 'began as an ass, became a philosopher, and is now an ass again. He showed us the Way, gave us the Book and the Stone, and we don't need him anymore.'

'I was an ass when I wrote that book, I'm a philosopher *now*! By the way, where do you get it?'

'Where do we get what?'

'The Vegetable Stone.'

'We learnt to prepare it and grow it ourselves, by following the method in the Book.'

Christian gapes like a stunned fish. 'You've upset him now' says O'Hara. '*He* can't make the Vegetable Stone, which proves he didn't write the book. Now then, to more serious charges. I understand (a) you've been telling people *real* baptism involves holding an adult under water till he's half drowned and then reviving him; and (b) that John the Baptist could be recognized by his big biceps and strong lungs.'

'That's what it says in Our Noble Book.'

'Where can I get a copy?' asks Adam.

The redheaded heretic gets the full treatment, dunce's cap and all. 'The cruellest thing ever we saw' complain the townspeople. 'A common criminal, sentenced to death, is made drunk for the execution, but this poor man is denied his harmless liquor substitute. Disgraceful!'

Before the stake, Inquisitor and heretic face each other for the last time on earth. All the fire's gone from Christian, in the face of his heretic's temeritous resolve.

'Can't you admit you made a mistake?' pleads Christian. 'It's not too late.'

'No' says the heretic, 'I'm happy to die for the Brotherhood. Survival's not important.'

'Yes it is' says Christian.

'No it's not' says the heretic.

'I used to feel as you now feel' says Christian, 'but you never felt as I. Doesn't that prove me the wiser of we two?'

'It would, if the world were flat.'

'You must *realize* it's round' says Christian, 'but you must *know* it's flat!'

'Light the faggots' says O'Hara.

'Please recant' implores Christian.

'Too late' shouts the heretic. 'I've learnt the Power of Truth!'

'Great' shouts Christian, 'Telling the Truth is the first part of Our Art. But the second is having something worth saying!'

'And the third aagh . . .'

'I haven't got to that, but I expect it's the point where the Lamb who doesn't exist but should, and the Wolf who shouldn't exist but does . . .'

Crackle. Adam collapses.

'Quick' sighs Christian. 'Get the boy clear of the flames, or he'll go up as well.'

Adam doesn't speak for a while. 'That heretic had great power' he says eventually. 'I think he put a spell on you.'

'Oh don't talk to me like that' says Christian, 'I'm a scientist! An Aristotelian scientist. That is to say, my science is wrong.'

'By the way Adam, did you know I got knocked back on the mortgage for that castle I fancied? Eighty-three years for essential repairs.'

28

Another trial draws to a close. 'You don't love me' complains the heretic.

'I *do* love you' says Christian, 'I love you so much I want you to see your error.'

'Then why not let me do it in my own good time? After all, as you say in the book, the chief error in this Art is haste.'

'The *chief* error, says Christian, 'is not the *only* error.'

'Hurrah' shouts Adam.

'Shut up' says O'Reilly. 'Don't get too cheeky, Adam: it has the same effect as not being cheeky at all.'

'I'll wake up to myself in time' says the heretic. 'After all; you did.'

'I'm exceptional' explains Christian. 'Not like you at all.'

'I had a dream last night, says Adam. 'I saw a group of serfs, oppressed, hungry, penniless, and before them a prelate, eating a feast. His hands were fat, like Father O'Reilly's, and on his fingers he wore ten rings.'

'The vision's equivocal' says Christian. 'It doesn't say whether you're prelate or serf.'

'How typical' says Adam. 'All *you* see is yourself. Living with you's an education!'

'I wish it were' says Christian. 'Now watch what I'm doing here. I take these yellow crystals, and when I heat them up, they disappear.'

'Sublimation' says Adam. 'How boring. From an earth to an air direct.'

'I can't understand you, Adam' sighs Christian. 'Don't you want to learn to make gold? You'll never own a castle, without a flaw in your personality. And how will you get to Heaven?'

'I'd like to see what gold there is divided fairly' says Adam. 'And in a just society, we'd have no need of religion.'

'The trouble with *your* generation' says Christian, 'you're far too conservative! You're only interested in what gold there is: the idea is to make more.'

O'Hara returns the latest transcript to the notary 'I reckon we're due for a switch in polarity. Signal to noise it down to blazes, which means zealous crusaders will soon give way to paranoic apostates. Hard to say who are the bigger nuisance.'

Deserted by their staff, riding camels confiscated from heretics, the team, minus O'Reilly, ride north. O'Hara curses softly, the notary is drunk, and Adam rides behind Christian. Disturbing the sylvan quiet with the coughing of their camels, through Aquitaine and France they ride.

'Tell me more about Wycliffe' says Adam to O'Hara, who wishes he'd never spoken.

'Where are we now?'

'The Holy Roman Empire. No new buildings, no trade on the highways, and I've counted seventy-two men nailed by their ears to posts since we left the woods.'

'We'll stop at the next town and make inquiries' says Christian. 'I'm tired of eating pinecones.'

The rain is pouring as they ride into town. The camels won't fit under the trees. The notary gets tangled up, and has to be assisted by a burgher with a goitre and a hare lip. The streets are awash with mud, the houses are made of rotten wood and crumbling stone. Everyone bathes on Saturday night, and it's Friday afternoon.

By the Christmas tree hangs a man in chains, two mastiffs gnawing his heels: Germany.

'What's he done?' asks Adam. 'Probably stole a crust of bread.'

They get to the inn in time for dinner, which is served from five to nine. You sit down at five and get up at nine; a law prohibits sitting at table for longer than five hours at a stretch.

Christian stands behind Adam in the queue for the fresh fish; these are housed in a wooden tank, and supplied with running water from a window.

'I'm going to ask what that man did' says Adam, munching a slab of salt-soaked bread.

'I'll preach a sermon against cruelty' promises Christian. 'Tomorrow or the next day.'

'What about a sermon against drink?' says Adam. 'I haven't seen a sober man in weeks!'

The village priest, glimpsing Christian, lays down a pudding the size of a man's leg, and rising from his table, a wooden three-decker groaning with cabbage and roast pork, walks over. 'There's something I wanted to ask you Brother: we have an adulteress here, caught in the act, and want to drown her in a sack with a cat, a cock, a snake and a dog. The trouble is, we can't find a cock; they've all been eaten. Would it be all right to use a surrogate? The mayor has a weather vane he uses for a doorstop.'

'Tell him the one about the woman taken in adultery' says Adam.

'I don't know that one' says Christian. 'Besides, this is hardly the time or place. A sense of humour is a wonderful thing – I wish I had one – but in the right context.'

'A sense of humour is the first part of Our Art' says Adam. 'That's the part we're better off without.'

'I'll be discussing these and related matters at my inquiry, says Christian, dismissing the priest. 'Right now, I want to satisfy my inner man: catch me the one with no green stuff on its gills.'

The trial begins a week later, the defendants three itinerant Beghards, male lay mendicants of dubious orthoxody, generally ignored by the Holy See. O'Hara knows he can rely on them railing against the Church, in the absence of knights.

'Once more' says O'Hara, 'for the gathered townfolk.'

'The Church is corrupt' says the eldest Beghard, a wraith-like, carious figure in strong contrast to the corpulent townspeople. 'The Church is in decay. The sacraments are the root of all evil, and anyway, poisons are on sale that render them obsolete.'

'Where would you get the gold to buy them?' says Christian. 'How would you know?'

'They give them away in Orleans' says the Beghard. 'In some cases, force them on you.'

'How old is that boy?' asks Christian, changing tack.

'Twelve' says the eldest Beghard.

'Disgraceful' says Christian. 'A boy that age should never be given the Stone!'

'It depends on his personality.'

'If he starts on the Stone at that age' says Christian, 'he'll never *develop* a personality.'

'He knows what we're talking about', says the Beghard boy, 'he's corrupt too.'

Christian smiles. Nice style of a boy, he thinks to himself. Ah well.

'The sacraments are surely the root of all evil' says Christian, 'but they're also the root of all virtue. You've thrown the baby out with the bathwater.'

'At least they don't worship the bathwater' says Adam.

'Strike that off the record, please notary.'

'What record?' says the notary 'I've got the cramp.'

* * *

The court adjourns for dinner, but debate continues at the inn. In the absence of the secular arm, there's no way to prevent the accused accompanying their accusers to table, and making a nuisance of themselves. The Inquisitors sit at a table to themselves; normally reserved for the hangman, it's a small three-decker job, groaning with sauerkraut and pork.

'Can I have that pickle' says the youngest Beghard to Adam, who tosses it over.

'The sacraments of marriage and the eucharist' continues Christian . . .

'Sex and veges' says the notary. 'Use language they understand, to save time.'

'All right, sex and veges, have no meaning for you . . .'

'Sex and veges?' says the youngest Beghard. 'Never heard of them. Can I have another pickle?'

'. . . because you robbed the Rosegarden! All you see now is toad, not eagle, and all you discuss is what you want to avoid.'

'We *are* opposed to everything' admit the Beghards, eldest and middle.

'Never oppose or embrace' says Christian. 'Learn from the example of Dominic and Francis. Regard all things with equanimity. After all, what does "The Stone is good" share with "The Stone is bad"?'

'They're both half truths?'

'Precisely. O'Hara! This man loves what he hates and hates what he loves: he's hip.'

'I know' says O'Hara. 'The first part of the Art – correct me if I'm wrong, Christian – is unconscious and undeliberate. The first direction to the novice is not, make yourself black, but stop what you're doing. Unfortunately, making yourself white is conscious and deliberate. The third part of the Art adds the villain's lack of deliberation to the neophyte's acquired merit.'

'And how is that done?' asks the middle Beghard.

'*You* don't do it' says O'Hara, 'it happens, if at all, by Grace! The so-called *Art* is preaching the truth, while reserving its use for others.'

'Not always' says Christian, tucking into a big round plate of fish. 'You make a mistake in rejecting the sacraments, because they're open to abuse. Just because something can be abused, doesn't mean it can't be used – on the contrary! The majority always spoil things for the minority; take a look at a fallow field.'

'He's the son of a count' says Adam, to his opposite number. 'Would you have guessed?'

'So you reckon the poison can be used properly' says the eldest Beghard.

'Er ah, pass the cheese.'

'Very doctrinaire' says O'Hara, polishing off his third plate of sauerkraut. 'Correct use of a sacrament implies transformation of something evil into a token affirmative gesture. Take the eucharist, for example.'

'I have' says the middle Beghard, 'and I never got high on a consecrated wafer yet.'

'It's all in the mind' says Christian. 'I once got high on a plate of dirt. But take marriage, if you like.'

'Wait a minute' says O'Hara, 'you're not implying there's a function for sex?'

'Er no, I wouldn't go as far as that.'

'Good' says the Beghard. 'We agree on something. I think that calls for a drink.'

'Come on' says the innkeeper, 'five hours is up! You mendicants are abusing my hospitality!'

'All right' says O'Hara. He makes a brave effort to get out the door unassisted, but falls in the fish tank on the opposite side of the room.

'Tell me' says Christian, supported on either side by a Beghard. 'What are ordinary people like?'

'Not bad' says the middle Beghard. 'We'd be more inclined to laugh about you with them, than laugh about them with you.'

'Please don't laugh on my account' says Christian, 'I regard them with equanimity. Mind you, that's not the same thing as indifference. The chief error in this Art is confusing the two.'

'In that book you wrote . . .' says the eldest Beghard.

'The fact is' says Christian, 'I didn't write that book; it was written by another personality of mine. Besides, the chief error in this Art is not haste, it is dogmatism.'

'Woof woof' says Adam.

'Whew' says Christian, 'I don't feel good. Now then: Court come to order! Guilty, sentenced to burn, but I can't find the matches. Released with a caution.'

'Here here' says O'Hara. He's flat on his back, holding a broken candle in his teeth.

'Dogmatism' says Christian to Adam, 'I suppose you wonder what that means. It means refusing to change your mind, when circumstances demand it.'

'I know another name for that' says Adam.

'No doubt you do' says Christian. 'Now then, who's going to teach me a popular song?'

Adam smiles at the younger Beghard. 'Find your brew' he says, 'then take the pot off the stove. See what happens when your pot boils over? You don't need a new *pot,* you need a new *stove.*'

29

They ride on to Regensburg in Bavaria, losing the notary on the way: he's taken up Harry Hotspur's offer of a campaign against the Lollards. Wycliffe's ideas have spread from England to Bohemia, and without an escort of Teutonic knights O'Hara dare proceed no further.

Arriving in Regensburg, they find their way blocked, to their annoyance, by a large crowd. 'Isn't he *handsome*' the people exclaim. 'He's all we heard and more!'

Christian turns scarlet. 'Cut it out' he says. 'You can be as I am, I'll teach you how.'

'Not *you*' says a woman, 'you shut your mouth. It's the *boy* we've heard so much of. Adam Cadman! And here he is! All they claim, and more!'

Adam dismounts, and surrounded by admirers, heads for the nearest cakeshop.

'I'm the one who spent years in the east' protests Christian, but no one is listening.

'There' says O'Hara. 'This is the church we've been allocated in Regensburg.'

'It's a wreck' says Christian. 'Ruined. Finished. Dangerous. Had its day.'

'We'll patch up the walls' says O'Hara, 'find a floor, build a roof, she'll be good as new. There's nothing wrong with this church that can't be mended with a little time and effort.'

'Well come on Christian, get down off your horse!'

Christian can't get down off his horse; the effort seems hardly worthwhile. He can't speak, can't move a muscle. He stares, as though in a dream. He sees it all, it stretches before him, strangling speech in his throat.

Three days later the master of the Preachers' Order rides into town from the south. At the same time, the master of the Rosicrucian Brotherhood rides into town from the west. After strained and hurried consultation with O'Hara, they meet by moonlight in the ruined church, where Christian, sitting on a broken joist, hardly seems to notice their presence. Preacher and heretic sit down together, united by mutual foe – Christian. The preacher is dressed in black and white, the heretic in red and gold.

The preacher speaks first. 'When, against my better judgement, I agreed with the Pope you be freed, it was on the understanding you had undergone a complete reversal of character. Judging by the transcripts of the trials I've seen, such is far from the case.'

'We' says the heretic, 'welcomed your apostasy, for as you write in the Book, a truth may often be felt with more force, in its absence, than in its presence. Who better than our noble father, to chastise and rebuke? To us, you had merely abandoned one form of teaching for another. But the Son must kill the Father in this Work, and you place the knife in my hand!'

'I was rather hoping you wouldn't want him killed' says the preacher, 'for that was what I had in mind. If, in condemning your founder to death I satisfy your ends, I must decline to do it.'

'There's truth on both sides' mumbles Christian. 'Neither one of you is entirely right, or completely wrong.'

In the silence that follows this admission of moral imbecility, a firearm is heard being primed.

'It is I' shouts Adam, from the eastern wall. '*None* of you deserves to survive. Religion and heresy are only gimmicks to keep men's minds off the issues!'

'Wrong' says Christian, 'Religion is a valid way of looking at the world, Adam. It's the method of choice when events are out of hand and kicking you up the arse. When you're in control, doing the kicking, you tend to become logical.'

'Then tell me this' says Adam. 'Why does religion like to see us in misery?'

'It's a question of how to keep the boy under the bed after the thunder has passed by. And don't you realize how old-fashioned it is to be ahead of your time?'

Adam fires his fowling piece, aiming to kill them all. He misses, but his shot ricochets, and wounds a passer-by. Preacher and heretic race off in hot pursuit of Adam, who grabs a horse and heads for the Bohemian border posthaste.

Christian, meantime, is filled with a sudden desire to revisit his childhood. He learns, on inquiring the next day, that his ancestral home is not far off. Imagine his delight, on arriving there, to find the castle derelict: he resolves to spend the rest of his life putting it in repair. Far from brooding over the events of his first twenty-three years, he never gives them a thought. If anyone mentions, after the Council of Constance in 1419, the Bohemian republic, Christian, the Comte de Rosencreutz, confesses himself confused as the next fellow. By judicious speculation he acquires a modest income, and spends the remaining years of his life, till his death in 1483, keeping fit, playing the harpsichord, cultivating bulbs, arguing with his neighbour over who should build the new boundary fence, and striving to improve the local breed of dog.

He has lots of worries, and like most of his kind, is visited by troublesome dreams. In one recurrent dream, he is standing alone by a gate, of which he appears to be keeper, wondering whether or not to admit an angel, dressed as a rose. The angel smiles at him, then suddenly slams the gate shut in his face.

'You have exhausted two of the three paths open to you' says the angel. 'The fourth is a consuming way. Know well, that if you fail in your third and final attempt, you will fail entirely, and the Mystery of That Which I Am, and That Which I Guard, will be lost to you always. At present, you sleep: but when you wake, you will carry the burden with you, in the form of lechery and constipation, of the paths you have trodden and failed. And when you fail the second path – for it is written you shall – in your rage you will destroy the second path, for all Christians, for all time. For you will so divide that path, and the division will so divide again, the path will become a maze. And the first path is dangerous, and the third given to few.'

Christian, whenever he wakes from this nightmare and finds his bowels open, wisely discounts it, and searches instead for the day-to-day problem that may have prompted it. He knows that dreaming is only important when reality takes a turn for the worse, and the more dreaming that's done, of course, the worse the turn that reality takes.

It's often some trivial, vexatious thing: indigestion; a slight at cards; insubordination from serfs; blocked drains; wet fuel. As soon as matters are set to rights, the dream promptly recedes, while the Reformation of the Whole Wide World, or part thereof, is accomplished.

It never occurs to Count Rosencreutz, in this life or the next, to ask himself what might be done to generalize such happiness. This will fall to the Child of another Age, though strictly speaking, there are but two ages, and two children; Christian the Cause, and Adam the Effect.

Cause is killed by Effect in this Work; thereafter, the Two mingle, and become One.

MORE ABOUT PENGUINS, PELICANS AND PUFFINS

For further information about books available from Penguins please write to Dept EP, Penguin Books Ltd, Harmondsworth, Middlesex UB7 0DA.

In the U.S.A.: For a complete list of books available from Penguins in the United States write to Dept DG, Penguin Books, 299 Murray Hill Parkway, East Rutherford, New Jersey 07073.

In Canada: For a complete list of books available from Penguins in Canada write to Penguin Books Canada Limited, 2801 John Street, Markham, Ontario L3R 1B4.

In Australia: For a complete list of books available from Penguins in Australia write to the Marketing Department, Penguin Books Australia Ltd, P.O. Box 257, Ringwood, Victoria 3134.

In New Zealand: For a complete list of books available from Penguins in New Zealand write to the Marketing Department, Penguin Books (N.Z.) Ltd, Private Bag, Takapuna, Auckland 9.

In India: For a complete list of books available from Penguins in India write to Penguin Overseas Ltd, 706 Eros Apartments, 56 Nehru Place, New Delhi 110019.

A CHOICE OF PENGUINS

☐ **_Small World_ David Lodge** £2.50

A jet-propelled academic romance, sequel to *Changing Places*. 'A new comic débâcle on every page' – *The Times.* 'Here is everything one expects from Lodge but three times as entertaining as anything he has written before' – *Sunday Telegraph*

☐ **_The Neverending Story_ Michael Ende** £3.95

The international bestseller, now a major film: 'A tale of magical adventure, pursuit and delay, danger, suspense, triumph' – *The Times Literary Supplement*

☐ **_The Sword of Honour Trilogy_ Evelyn Waugh** £3.95

Containing *Men at Arms, Officers and Gentlemen* and *Unconditional Surrender*, the trilogy described by Cyril Connolly as 'unquestionably the finest novels to have come out of the war'.

☐ **_The Honorary Consul_ Graham Greene** £2.50

In a provincial Argentinian town, a group of revolutionaries kidnap the wrong man . . . 'The tension never relaxes and one reads hungrily from page to page, dreading the moment it will all end' – Auberon Waugh in the *Evening Standard*

☐ **_The First Rumpole Omnibus_ John Mortimer** £4.95

Containing *Rumpole of the Bailey, The Trials of Rumpole* and *Rumpole's Return*. 'A fruity, foxy masterpiece, defender of our wilting faith in mankind' – *Sunday Times*

☐ **_Scandal_ A. N. Wilson** £2.25

Sexual peccadillos, treason and blackmail are all ingredients on the boil in A. N. Wilson's new, *cordon noir* comedy. 'Drily witty, deliciously nasty' – *Sunday Telegraph*

A CHOICE OF PENGUINS

☐ ***Stanley and the Women*** **Kingsley Amis** £2.50

'Very good, very powerful ... beautifully written ... This is Amis *père* at his best' – Anthony Burgess in the *Observer*. 'Everybody should read it' – *Daily Mail*

☐ ***The Mysterious Mr Ripley*** **Patricia Highsmith** £4.95

Containing *The Talented Mr Ripley*, *Ripley Underground* and *Ripley's Game*. 'Patricia Highsmith is the poet of apprehension' – Graham Greene. 'The Ripley books are marvellously, insanely readable' – *The Times*

☐ ***Earthly Powers*** **Anthony Burgess** £4.95

'Crowded, crammed, bursting with manic erudition, garlicky puns, omnilingual jokes ... (a novel) which meshes the real and personalized history of the twentieth century' – Martin Amis

☐ ***Life & Times of Michael K*** **J. M. Coetzee** £2.95

The Booker Prize-winning novel: 'It is hard to convey ... just what Coetzee's special quality is. His writing gives off whiffs of Conrad, of Nabokov, of Golding, of the Paul Theroux of *The Mosquito Coast*. But he is none of these, he is a harsh, compelling new voice' – Victoria Glendinning

☐ ***The Stories of William Trevor*** £5.95

'Trevor packs into each separate five or six thousand words more richness, more laughter, more ache, more multifarious human-ness than many good writers manage to get into a whole novel' – *Punch*

☐ ***The Book of Laughter and Forgetting***
  Milan Kundera £3.95

'A whirling dance of a book ... a masterpiece full of angels, terror, ostriches and love ... No question about it. The most important novel published in Britain this year' – Salman Rushdie

KING PENGUIN

☐ *The White Hotel* D. M. Thomas

'A major artist has once more appeared', declared the *Spectator* on the publication of this acclaimed, now famous novel which recreates the imagined case history of one of Freud's woman patients.

☐ *Just Relations* Rodney Hall

A tiny, remote Australian community unites to thwart progress – 'It's farce, it's comedy, it's tragedy, it's grotesque and tender and dreadful and full of wisdom' – *Times* (Canberra).

☐ *A Time to Dance* Bernard Mac Laverty

Ten stories, including 'My Dear Palestrina' and 'Phonefun Limited', by the author of *Cal*: 'A writer who has a real affinity with the short story form' – *The Times Literary Supplement*

☐ *Keepers of the House* Lisa St Aubin de Terán

Seventeen-year-old Lydia Sinclair marries Don Diego Beltrán and goes to live on his family's vast, decaying Andean farm. This exotic and flamboyant first novel won the Somerset Maugham Award.

☐ *Transit of Venus* Shirley Hazzard

Two sisters emigrate to England from Australia in search of new lives. Through their lovers, marriages, jobs, children – and failures – a whole landscape of change and transit can be glimpsed. 'Sumptuous . . . impeccable' – *The Times* (London).

☐ *The Stories of William Trevor*

'Trevor packs into each separate five or six thousand words more richness, more laughter, more ache, more multifarious human-ness than many good writers manage to get into a whole novel' – *Punch*. 'Classics of the genre' – Auberon Waugh